KILL THEM QUICKLY

ED GRACE

Blood Splatter Press

For Dad.
Thanks for all your help.

BIRMINGHAM, ENGLAND

CHAPTER ONE

NATHANIEL'S FEATURES WERE LIKE HIS FATHER'S — WHEN they weren't beaten and mangled, that is.

Damien's heel lay into his ribs.

Wayne's crowbar knocked into his kneecap.

And when Simon and Raul, his father's final two lackeys joined in — well, let's just say Nathaniel's teeth lasted longer than his begging.

His father sat in his chair. At the end of the warehouse. Watching. Silent. Deliberate.

Always so deliberate.

That's what made his father so powerful. Not his control over the authorities, nor that he was already a high-ranking sergeant of his crime family by the time he was seventeen, and not even how doting and loyal every idiot he commanded was — it was the silence. The methodical deliberation to his every movement. The invisible anger that powered his actions.

"Enough."

The beating halted and the men stepped back, revealing what was left of Nathaniel. His suit, bought for him by his father on his eighteenth birthday a few months ago, was now ripped and torn. Hanging from his bones. Ripped and covered with bloody prints.

His father stood.

His name was Hugo Jones, and he walked slowly and particularly. The soles of his Berluti shoes were silent, yet the foreboding of his steps echoed around the warehouse.

"Please..." said Nathaniel. "Please, Dad, I–"

Hugo wasn't interested. He raised his boot and stamped on Nathaniel's nose. He'd told his lackeys to leave the nose for him and, following one plunge of his heel, that nose became cracked and bloody.

"Dad, don't believe them, it's not true!"

Hugo said nothing.

He never did. Not when silence could say everything for him.

Why speak when words only undermined you?

"Dad, they are full of shit, I didn't–"

"Nah, we ain't!" one of them objected, probably Wayne.

Hugo raised his hand, and Wayne ceased arguing.

"Dad, please," Nathaniel said, no longer shouting; instead trying a quiet whimper.

Hugo took the knife from the back of his Armani suit trousers. He withdrew his Saint Laurent Mesh Scarf handkerchief and wiped the glistening silver of the knife.

He held the knife up and squinted as the light emphasised its perfection.

"Dad, it's lies, all lies, I didn't, I mean, I wouldn't–"

Hugo crouched, casting a shadow over his son. In as quiet a voice as he could speak and still be heard, he responded with an aggressive softness no one could match.

"How long?" he asked.

"Dad, I haven't, I swear–"

Hugo flicked the leather handle of his knife and the blade disappeared into Nathaniel's thigh.

Hugo held it in, watching Nathaniel's face as it morphed into anguish. His son's screams reverberated throughout the vicinity. Hugo's face remained cold.

Hugo lifted the knife out.

Nathaniel lifted his body up, reaching toward his thigh, but dared not touch or comfort the wound. To do so would be to further disrespect his father. Hugo would expect the pain to be suffered and the bleeding to flow.

Hugo opened the handkerchief and rested the knife against it, wiping away blood that shared some of his DNA.

"How long?" he asked.

Nathaniel did not reply this time. He stared up at his father, caught between denying it and admitting it, not knowing which would exacerbate the situation further.

Hugo demanded a response with the raising of his eyebrows.

"Dad... Please... I didn't mean to..."

Hugo flicked the leather handle again, and this time the blade disappeared into Nathaniel's shoulder. Not in a place that would cause immediate fatal damage, but in a place where the pain would precede the slow process of bleeding out.

He retracted the knife. Wiped the blade. Waited for the screams to finish.

"Your mother will be so disappointed," Hugo muttered.

"What will she say when you kill me?" Nathaniel asked.

"She'll say, why did our son have to do something so stupid?"

"But, Dad, I–"

"I'm fifty-two years old, Nathaniel. I have lived many years, and with all the photographs they showed me, all the police who told me, all the rumours I heard, none of it was as strong evidence as my instinct: and my instinct tells me you are a dirty, little liar."

Hugo held the tip of the knife an inch from Nathaniel's eye.

3

"I will give you one more chance to come clean and answer my question," he said. "How long?"

Nathaniel stared at the knife.

His eyes widened, creating a larger target.

Sweat seeped down his cold forehead.

He took a big, deep breath, and his mouth opened.

"I was giving them stuff for fourteen months, but I swear it was only because—"

The blade entered Nathaniel's eye.

It didn't all go in at first, so Hugo had to push.

He pressed down on the handle with both hands, pushing it, putting all of his body weight into forcing it further and further, until it had pierced through Nathaniel's eye and entered his brain.

By the time Hugo stood and surveyed what he'd done, his son's body no longer moved.

"What a disappointment you were," Hugo said so quietly that only he and Nathaniel's corpse would hear. "I feel ashamed to call you my son."

He turned to the others.

Simon. Damien. Raul.

And Wayne.

Wayne, who had broken the news to him.

Hugo had wanted to kill Wayne just for providing the information, but knew he should be understanding. It would have been tough to tell a man like Hugo that his son was dirty.

Hugo walked up to Wayne, who stared back with wide eyes. He placed a hand around the back of Wayne's neck and pulled him close.

"Thank you," Hugo said.

Wayne nodded.

Hugo let go and turned back to his son.

The empty body in a pool of blood.

The heir to a legacy he did not deserve.

"Where was he hiding?" Hugo asked.

The others looked to each other, as if daring the other to talk. Hugo did not stop staring at his son.

"Frome," Simon answered.

"Where in Frome?"

"With a farmer called Connor and his wife. And their granddaughter. On a farm."

"And did this man know that Nathaniel was my son?"

Simon looked to the others for clarification. They did not look at him.

"I don't think so."

"Why don't you think so?"

Simon shrugged. "I think the man just took him in out of the kindness of his heart."

Hugo sighed.

"Fool," he said.

He looked away from his son and added, "Kill them."

Hugo turned to leave.

"Boss?" Wayne asked, and Hugo paused.

Hugo did not turn around. He just waited.

"Do you want us to kill all of them? I mean, the old man let him in. Do you want his wife and granddaughter done too?"

Hugo paused. Considered this.

"The old man and the wife." He went to leave, then paused, realising he could make quite a bit of money out of an orphaned girl. "Bring the granddaughter to me."

He left.

The rest of them breathed a sigh of relief.

Once they had cleared up Nathaniel's mess, they would be on their way to Frome, ready to do their job.

PRAGUE, CZECH REPUBLIC

CHAPTER TWO

İT WAS A BEAUTIFUL CITY. WARM. SCENIC. BY THE VLTAVA River, a surface of clear blue in the way few rivers still have. The city's history was turbulent, but that only amplified its present beauty. It had become a city of culture. Of tourism.

The Prague Astronomical Clock.

Old Town Square.

The Jewish Quarter.

Places people came from all over the world to see.

Or so you'd think.

In truth, the city was full of stag parties here for the cheap beer. A pint here was less than a pound, meaning they could get pissed for a little amount of money.

It disgusted Daniel Heal how so many people could tarnish the city's beauty for cheap thrills. It was like someone admiring the Mona Lisa because they liked the frame.

Looking out of the window of his flat, he contemplated his recent move. He and his ex-wife's relationship had been difficult for a while. His decision to relocate to another country and start a new job without her hadn't been an easy one to make.

Yet it had been an easy decision for her to accept.

She hadn't even put up a fight. No objections, no refuting, no *are you not even going to fight for us?*

It was as if marriage counselling and long conversations and silent dinner tables had worn away at her, and all that was left was the woman he used to call his wife, so far from who she once was.

Had he destroyed that woman?

He shook his head. Of course not. Two people were responsible for destroying that marriage.

His job had always been the priority; it had to be. Maybe she understood that, and that's why she didn't fight. A chance to work at the embassy, doing important work for the government...

No matter how much he thought about it, he never found any answers. So he just stood, allowing his mind to wander over petty arguments and misunderstandings.

The entire time he stood there, gazing out the window, his mind meandering down dark paths, he had no idea he was being watched.

He had no idea that Jay Sullivan had entered this room hours before Daniel had returned home. That Jay Sullivan had looked for potential weapons Daniel could use. That he had prepared his assassination.

When Daniel went to make dinner, he would find no kitchen knives in the drawer, no corkscrew by his wine, and no heavy utensils in the cupboards. There would be nothing he could use to defend himself.

But he needn't worry; he would not make it that far. No one did when Jay Sullivan lurked in their shadow. Unnoticed. Waiting for the right time. Waiting for the moment he could confirm the kill and receive his payment.

And this was his opportune moment.

As Daniel decided he had ruminated enough, he moved

away from the window. Sullivan stepped forward, placed a hand on Daniel's throat, and pushed him backwards until he pressed against the wall.

The knife was in Daniel's throat before he had registered what was happening.

Sullivan looked into the eyes of his target as he held the knife in Daniel's oesophagus. He felt nothing for him. He wouldn't be much of an assassin if he did.

Once the time was right, Sullivan removed the knife and dropped Daniel to the floor.

Sullivan stood still, waiting for the wriggling to stop. For the suffering to end.

One may feel sorry for someone like Daniel in this situation, but Sullivan didn't.

Daniel was up to a lot of bad things, so the Falcons must have instructed Sullivan to kill Daniel for the right reasons.

Not that Sullivan knew those reasons. He just knew who to kill, how, and when.

They taught him that the reasons were not important. He did not need them to perform his job.

Daniel stopped moving.

Sullivan crouched. Placed two fingers on the man's neck.

No pulse.

It was done.

He stood. Turned. Ready to make his way through his planned exit route.

But a sight he did not expect to encounter stopped him.

They had told him Daniel Heal would be alone.

They had told him there would be no one else to deal with.

They had not told him that, when Daniel separated from his wife a few months ago, he had gained custody of his son.

And there he stood.

In his pyjamas.

Couldn't be older than six or seven.

Frozen stiff. Like weeds had burst out of the ground and held him in place.

The kid pissed himself.

He had planets on his pyjamas. A teddy in his arm. A wet patch running down his leg.

Shit.

Sullivan had not been told to kill a child.

But he had also been told not to leave any witnesses.

He flexed his fingers over the knife.

Drew breath.

And stepped toward the child.

That's when a bouncer shoved Sullivan's shoulder and he woke up. The dream, conjured from the darkest recesses of his memory, faded as he was kicked out of another bar.

FROME, ENGLAND

CHAPTER THREE

THE FEELING OF NAUSEA DID NOT BOTHER JAY SULLIVAN.

Unfortunately, it was a frequent occurrence of his evenings. He spent most of his nights feeling like he would be sick. To exist was to be on the edge of vomiting.

He would protest that he was not an alcoholic, he just had nothing better to do. Why feel his pain when he could numb it instead? Why allow the guilt from many years of murder to surface when he could drink such feelings away?

Somehow, Sullivan had ended up on the streets of Frome, a rural town in the southwest of England. He wasn't sure why he was there, but he hardly aimed to arrive anywhere anymore; he would just travel and see where life took him. If he didn't know where he was going, neither would anyone else.

He'd never been to Frome, which was odd. He'd been to most countries, but never to this quaint little place. The streets were cobbled and hilly, and most shops were gift shops or independent cafes.

It was the kind a town someone may retire to, or a friendly farmer may work the field, or a happy couple might buy their dream home. It was not the place for a once legendary government assassin who had crumbled after losing his daughter. He had found his daughter, only to watch her kill his only friend and disappear once again; leaving him to live out the rest of his days in content misery.

He still wore a suit. Why not? He had enough money left over from his days of assassinations that he could afford enough expensive suits to fill a house. He may as well attempt to look the part, even if he did not feel the part. Yes, he could still beat someone in a fight, and yes, he still had the assassin's mindset; it was hard to lose — every time he walked into a room he still found his mind unconsciously looking for objects he could use for weapons, and checking for potential assailants. But his glory days were gone now. He did not consider himself worth the status he'd attained anymore; but the suit could almost convince him otherwise. It could make him feel as brilliant as he once was, back when he experienced the rush of a perfectly executed kill. He was known as 'the assassin without a gun.' He'd never needed one — he'd kill a target with something from their environment. Their child's toy, the hot tap in the bathroom — hell, he'd executed many targets with their own fountain pens.

Could he still do that now?

Why would he need to?

Once, it mattered. The Falcons paid him — a secret government organisation that employed him, then betrayed him.

But he didn't want to hurt anyone anymore. He'd spent his life killing targets they had told him deserved their death. He'd been taught not to question it. That was until they labelled him a target to cover their own mistakes.

Now they had a truce. A *you don't screw with me, I don't screw with you* kind of deal.

Then again, was it a truce? Or was he such little threat anymore that they'd forgotten about him?

He'd might have felt bad for being forgotten, but all he felt at that moment was drunk. Queasy and unstable. Stumbling and bumbling and, hey, who left this bench here?

In the darkness, his eyes did not pick up the bench well enough to avoid its impact on his kneecap.

It hurt.

He grew angry. Went to fight the bench. The bench now his greatest enemy. Then he realised: it was a bench. So instead of fighting it, he slumped down on it. Allowed his head to fall and dangle over the bench's back.

The stars above shone down, like a million galaxies judging him.

Why was he even still bothering?

It was for one simple reason.

His daughter. Talia.

She was somewhere else, trying to find her place in this world, and he'd stayed alive in case she needed him again. The faintest of hopes that she may re-find him once she had figured out who she was.

He went to lift his beer to his lips.

He didn't have one.

A shriek drew his attention. His face lifted, and his muscle pulled as he rotated his neck toward the source of the sound.

It was coming from a nearby alleyway.

A bunch of teenagers were being noisy. Burberry caps. Collars up. Tracksuits.

Ah, yes. It was *this* kind of teenager.

His father was a police officer and refused to let him become one of *those* teenagers.

That's how his father had referred to them.

Those.

Each mention of these uncivilised yobs would prompt an upward turn of his nostrils, and a silent judgement screaming from his frown.

Then Sullivan turned sixteen, and his dad shot his wife and

himself. So, honestly, Sullivan didn't concern himself with the man's judgement.

Still, Sullivan didn't need to intervene. It was late, and they were causing trouble, but it didn't affect him. He was content to remain slumped in his intoxicated stupor.

Then that screech came again.

Sullivan looked up, and that's when he realised.

Those teenagers were surrounding a cat.

He squinted against — well, nothing, no light at all in fact; Sullivan just squinted – and he saw between their legs. A black cat was trying to get away, but was unable to because of the tubes stuck to its legs. One of the teenagers spray-painted the cat yellow.

Sullivan didn't know what he was doing. Before he'd consciously acknowledged his decision, his legs had staggered him to the alleyway, and he was within metres of the scumbags.

One of them nudged another and nodded in Sullivan's direction. With cocky smirks, they turned to him.

There were three.

All of them arrogant. Each one another useless drain on society. Each one undeserving of what they had.

He readied his fist, then paused.

Fuck. What am I doing?

The cat tried to get away, but the kid with the spray-paint kicked it over and held it down with his foot.

"You ain't going nowhere," he said.

"Let the–" Sullivan hiccupped — "cat go."

They laughed.

They would laugh, wouldn't they? They wouldn't know who this guy was. They'd think it was some drunken vigilante-wannabe who was about to get beaten up.

"You wanna get shanked, bruv?" one of them asked.

Sullivan grimaced. The boy's use of semantics was irritating. This kid knew nothing of 'shanking'. Sullivan had 'shanked' many people. At best, this kid had scared a few other kids at school. Also, if he had a knife he would supposedly be 'shanking' Sullivan with, why hadn't he taken it out?

Spray-Paint Kid pressed the sole of his trainer harder against the cat's belly and grinned at Sullivan.

Sullivan stepped forward. Hesitated.

He could beat the hell out of these guys pretty easily. With little effort, he would smack the first guy's head against the nearby dumpster, break the second guy's neck with a well-struck fist, and impale the final one's neck on the exposed nail a few metres down to his left.

But then what?

Was he capable of stopping there?

He was drunk. He wasn't in control. And even if he was in control, he wasn't sure he'd have the sense to stop once he started.

Bastards or not, he didn't want to kill people anymore.

He sighed. Backed away from them.

"This dickhead ain't serious!"

"Yo bruv, you ain't going nowhere. Don't start shit you ain't gonna finish."

The first one stepped forward and swung a fist. It was a poorly lunged fist. The delinquent had thrown all of his body with it, so he was leaning top heavy. It was a fist thrown by someone with no training; the guy was off balance straight away, and it allowed Sullivan to easily swipe the fist away then stick his leg out and trip him up.

The next one came at him with no clear intention of what he would do. The way he charged, it was as if he'd given no thought whatsoever to his strategy. Sullivan struck his fist into the guy's face before his flailing arms had reached him.

"Oh, you gettin' it!" said the first one as he stood.

Sullivan grabbed his neck and pushed him against the wall.

The scumbag fought against it, punching and striking at

Sullivan's arms. His face reddened. He wheezed. His thrashing became weaker.

Sullivan realised what he was doing.

He loosened his grip.

The cat ran away, somehow free of the cardboard tubes.

He looked to the three teenage fools. The cat had run away; that was his purpose for confronting them. He needn't be there anymore.

He turned to leave, but they dragged him back.

"You ain't going nowhere."

He paused.

He had to fight. They would not let him go.

But if he fought them, what then? How would he stop himself from killing them? Even if he just knocked them around a bit, without thinking, he might throw them against that exposed nail poking off the wall and...

And then what?

There was no way he could be sure he wouldn't fatally hurt them. He'd been trained to punch the places of the body most likely to cause death. What if he threw that punch by instinct? He didn't want to kill anyone.

The only thing he could do was take it.

Sullivan's chest screamed.

He had a heart problem. He took out a few pills and swallowed them dry.

"Look at this guy, he's so limp he has to take pills."

He sighed. One of them punched his cheek. It was weak. It made him flinch.

Another punched, then another joined in.

Someone hit him from behind with the lid of a bin and he allowed it to push him to his knees. In a sudden wave of nausea, he was sick. A mass of bloody lumps lurched from his mouth and across the damp alley floor.

Feet and fists paraded upon him.

He lay on the floor of the alleyway and took it.

Was this what it took to be a good man? Allowing himself to take a beating to save their lives?

He closed his eyes and, eventually, whether from pain or alcohol — it didn't matter – he passed out, his consciousness drifting into absence.

CHAPTER FOUR

A PLEASANT AROMA OF FISH AND CHIPS WAFTED FROM THE bag in Connor's hand. Despite approaching his seventieth year, a chippy tea still gave him the same pleasure it gave him when he was a boy. He opened his car door and placed the bag on the passenger seat; but just as he was about to get in, something drew his attention.

A group of men, probably around nineteen or twenty, rushed across the street and into an alleyway. They were enthusiastic about something. As if someone was doing something incredible, and they wished to be that person's enthusiastic voyeur.

Connor couldn't help but look.

At the edge of the alleyway, the clump of teenagers and young men gathered. Between their ripped jeans and skinny trousers, someone was lying on the floor. In the middle of the gathering circle.

It took Connor a moment to realise it was a person. On the floor, in the middle of them, was a man, taking the beating of a lifetime. Bombarded by kicks and punches and stomps.

These young men were spending their evenings torturing someone less fortunate.

Connor remembered being a young man. It was quite a while ago now, but he remembered it. He would be up at five in the morning to work, and he wouldn't stop until at least seven that evening. He had not abused his privilege like this.

As he continued to stare, he realised he recognised one of them. Two of them, in fact. They were sons of the woman who ran the post office; a woman who would not be happy to know what her boys were up to.

He stepped forward and called out, "Billy. Jason. Is that you?"

One of them turned and looked at Connor, his eyes widening.

"Shit, let's go!"

The boy ran. His brother turned and saw Connor, so ran as well. The rest conformed, perhaps assuming the law had shown up rather than an old man, and they all dispersed.

Connor checked it was safe to cross the road and walked to the man's side.

The man's eyelids flickered. He had a cut on his face, appeared concussed, and his suit was in terrible shape. He was fairly out of it but could probably walk. Connor could take him to the hospital, but it was a long drive; besides, his wife used to be a nurse. She could help him.

"Come on," Connor said, and pulled the man up by the hand. The man's hand almost slipped out of Connor's, soaked by puddles of the alleyway, but after a struggle, Connor managed to help him up. Despite the aching it gave him, he helped this man limp to his car.

He replaced the man's suit blazer with the jacket on his shoulders and lay him down on the backseat.

He took to the driver's seat, breathing through twinges of his aching bones, wondering what this world had become.

23

CHAPTER FIVE

IT WOULD BE NICE TO SAY IT WAS THE BEAUTIFUL MORNING'S sunshine beaming through a crack in the curtains that awoke Sullivan, or that it was the enticing fragrance of bacon drifting from downstairs.

Unfortunately, it was neither.

It was the headache. The excruciating, pounding, twisting, grinding headache that dragged from the top of his head to the base of his skull.

He groaned, turning over, lifting a pillow over his ears. The pillow was soft and smelt of lavender, and it was a slight comfort. He squashed it over his head, pressing down until the pain lessened.

Hang on...

A pillow?

Smelling of lavender?

Sunlight through curtains?

Sullivan shoved the pillow aside and sat up. Looked around.

"What the hell..."

He was in a spacious room, with light blue painted walls and a grand wardrobe against the far wall. Floral curtains replicated the flower patterns of the comfortably heavy bedsheets.

On the bedside table was a glass of water.

He needed water. Desperately. It would go a long way to fighting his headache.

But who put the water there? What was in it?

Deciding he didn't care if it was poisoned, he took the glass of water, placed it against his lips, and gulped its entire contents down his throat.

Across the room was a chair. On it, some folded clothes. On that, a note.

He stepped out of the bed.

He was wearing just his underwear.

He wasn't sure whether to be surprised, offended, worried, or all three.

The note on top of the clothes read:

Your suit is being cleaned and should be ready for you soon. Meanwhile, these are some of my old clothes, and they should fit you. Please come down for breakfast when you are ready.

Did he fuck someone?

He felt dirty for wondering it, but it was the most obvious question. He tried thinking back to the previous night. He remembered a few teenagers and a cat, but little else.

But these were a man's clothes.

Unless alcohol had a severe effect upon his sexuality, a one-night stand made little sense.

Nevertheless, he wasn't prepared to confront what was downstairs in nothing but his haggard skin. He put on a slightly baggy pair of brown corduroy trousers and a checked shirt, along with thick thermal socks and some underwear.

Once he'd put these clothes on, deliberately avoiding his reflection in a vanity mirror on the cupboard, he opened the curtains and looked out.

Fields spread out before him. Below was a garden with a swing set, a Volkswagen Sharan, an empty tractor, a shed, and a child's popup football net. A few of the fields were full of corn, and one was home to a set of sheep.

Where the hell was he?

He went to the cupboard and opened the drawers. A few folded clothes, a belt, nothing particularly helpful. But there was a jewellery box. He opened it, and there was a pin, the kind that might hold a brooch. He readied its tip and edged to the door.

He pulled it open. Slowly. Peering out.

A corridor led to some stairs. Light conversation accompanied the smell of bacon and sound of frying.

He crept along the hallway until he reached the top of the stairs. Staying close to the bannister, and with his makeshift weapon hidden in his sleeve, he sneaked down.

The talking grew louder, though it wasn't particularly loud. He made out a man, a woman and a child. All talking about some television show or something. Sponge Bob, maybe.

Or maybe Sullivan was guessing Sponge Bob as it was the only kid's show he knew.

He edged along the wall, reaching the doorway, and looked in.

A man, past retirement age, stood at the stove. Scrambled egg in one pan, bacon frying on the other, something in another pan. Beans, maybe?

Attached to the kitchen was a dining area, with four plates on the dining table. A lady of similar age to the man sat with a girl, possibly ten or eleven.

This could all be fake. All be setup. It could be a trap.

But it was unlikely.

He put the hairpin into his back pocket. Took a deep breath. Stepped into the room.

"Good morning," said the man with a spritely voice. "I see you found the clothes I put out for you. They aren't the best-looking items I have, but they–"

"Where am I?"

The woman and the child stopped talking. They stared at him. The man plated the bacon.

"On my farm. It's near Frome, which is where I found you."

"Found me?"

"Yep."

"Why did you have to find me? Why couldn't you just leave me?"

The man served the scrambled egg and the beans, put the pans in the sink, then turned to Sullivan. He leant against the kitchen side, studying his new guest.

"You were drunk," the man answered.

"I am always drunk."

"You were in danger."

"I am always in — look, I can take care of myself. You don't know me. You don't know who I am."

"Well, you didn't look to be taking care of yourself all that well."

"Is this because of those kids? And that cat?"

The man frowned. "I don't know of any kids or cats, but you were taking quite a beating. You were concussed. I assumed you'd appreciate being rescued."

"Great," he muttered.

"Come," the man said. "I've made breakfast. Join us."

"I can't, I really should–"

"I don't like wasting bacon. Come."

The man took the first two plates to the table, placing them before the woman and the girl. He took the other two, placing

27

them before his seat, then one before an empty seat opposite him.

He nodded at the empty seat, and Sullivan found his legs unknowingly carrying him forward, steadily and slowly, until he sat down.

He did not tuck himself under. Nor did he pick up his knife and fork. Nor did he glance at his breakfast.

"Who are you?" he asked.

"My name is Connor," the man said. "This is my wife, Elsie, and this is my granddaughter, Cassy. Do you have a name?"

He looked at the granddaughter, who smiled at him sweetly.

She reminded him so much of Talia.

With that thought, he decided he needed to leave. Urgently.

"I have to go," Sullivan said.

"I've made breakfast. Please, I insist."

No, no, no. This was all wrong.

He couldn't hurt this family.

He would bring them nothing but pain. Terror always followed him; anguish and violence had twisted into his shadow. There was nothing he could do for these people other than put them in danger.

"I really need to go," Sullivan said, pushing his chair out, standing, backing away, looking around, searching for something although he wasn't sure what.

"What is so urgent?" asked Connor.

"You don't understand. I'm bad news. I will cause you nothing but trouble."

"Well, fortunately for you, trouble already has a way of finding us."

"Not this kind of trouble." Sullivan stood and turned toward the door. "I'm sorry."

"Where are you going to go? It's at least a five-mile walk until you get anywhere."

"I've walked farther."

"I'll drive you."

Sullivan paused. Turned back to the man.

"If you so wish," Connor continued, "I will drive you to wherever you need to go. But after we've finished breakfast. Then you can be on your way, if that's what you need."

"It's best for you if I go."

"I'm not in the habit of turning away troubled strangers. But, should you not wish for any further help from me, I can't stop you. But after breakfast. Please."

Connor held his hand toward the empty chair.

Reluctantly, Sullivan edged toward it and sat.

It was just breakfast.

That was all.

How much harm could he do to this family over breakfast?

He picked up his knife and fork, took the first bite, and realised how hungry he was. He rushed down the rest of his breakfast without saying another word.

CHAPTER SIX

It was the best breakfast Sullivan had eaten in a long time.

He had attended the classiest of restaurants for many of his meals — the money he had left from his killing days left him plenty to spend, and he hardly had his own kitchen to cook in. But there was something about a home-cooked breakfast, made with love for one's family, that a restaurant could never replicate. It felt warm and cared for — not in the manufactured way a chef may care about their restaurant, but in the way a grandfather cares about his family's happiness.

Sullivan's suit hung over a radiator. It hadn't dried yet, but Sullivan insisted that didn't matter. He took the plastic bag offered to him by Elsie and put his suit in that. He needed to leave before he brought any trouble to this family.

He needed the bathroom before he left. On the way, he glanced at framed pictures of Cassy, of Connor and Elsie in their younger days, and of a couple who had a strong familiarity to both Cassy and Connor.

"That was my daughter and her husband," came a voice from behind him.

Elsie stepped out of the bathroom, drying her hands with a towel.

Sullivan went to speak, but realised he had nothing to say. He stared at the pictures. She looked at him. It had been a while since he'd been around people who required real conversation — was he meant to say something here?

"They look happy," Sullivan said, his voice coming out hoarse and broken.

He reprimanded himself for the reply. What a stupid, pointless observation to make.

"They were," Elsie replied, as if there wasn't something odd about his comment. She returned the towel to the bathroom, then peered over Sullivan's shoulder at the photograph. Even though he knew this woman was not going to attack him, he did not like having someone behind him; so he stepped beside her.

"Were?" Sullivan asked.

"Nearly eight years ago now."

"What happened?"

"Car crash. Someone overtaking at sixty who didn't want to be stuck behind a truck. Head-on collision."

"Jesus."

Sullivan had seen head-on collisions. The wreckage normally left cars too squashed together for an intact human to remain. There was little chance anyone would survive.

"And Cassy?" Sullivan asked.

"She was too young. She doesn't remember them. Only vague images."

"I'm sorry."

"You don't need to be sorry, you didn't know them."

He looked at her. It was a fair point. He hadn't known them. He hadn't caused their deaths; he'd caused many, but they not theirs. There was no responsibility befalling him, so why was he saying he was sorry?

"Just feels like the right thing to say."

"Normally does."

"You take care of her now?"

"We do."

"Bet you're doing a great job."

"Well..." She shrugged her shoulders. "Best we can. We're old, in case you hadn't noticed. We have little energy to be chasing a child around, or disciplining her, or going bike riding with her, or to do any of the things a good parent should."

He snorted, but unnoticeably. If his father had gone a day without hitting him or his mother, Sullivan would have considered that a reward.

"She's always excited to have a guest here," Elsie said. "Means there's someone she can–"

"I'm not what you think I am."

"Excuse me?"

"I mean..." He had phrased that poorly. "I'm not a good person."

"Says who?"

Hundreds of corpses and mourning families.

"People."

"I judge someone by the actions I see, not the gossip I hear."

"You don't get it. I'm not a man you want around. I have nothing to offer you, and you certainly have nothing to offer me."

She smiled.

"You never told us your name," she observed.

He looked at her.

Paused.

She looked old but not haggard. She looked wrinkled, but not ruined. There was plenty of life left in this woman yet.

Sullivan did not plan on ruining that.

"I wish you the best of luck," said Sullivan, and walked past her, into the bathroom.

He stared vacantly as he went to the toilet, avoided his reflection as he washed his face, then made his way to the front door.

It was time he was leaving.

CHAPTER SEVEN

SULLIVAN LEFT THE HOUSE AND FELT THE GENTLE DRUMMING of raindrops patting his head. He paused. Looked over the fields disappearing into the distance.

The sky was grey, the fields were empty, and his body was tired. Yet nature had never looked as beautiful as it did on this farm.

"Dammit," said Connor.

"What?"

"I forgot my keys. Back in a moment."

He walked back inside the house, leaving Sullivan alone — or so he had thought. A poorly played guitar drew his attention.

He looked around, seeking its source. To his left was a barn, with open doors, where he found his feet wandering.

In there was the girl. Cassy. With an acoustic guitar, plucking at a few strings. From the chaotic order of notes, Sullivan could pick out *Twinkle Twinkle*.

She tried again and again to play it, but each time her first finger slid up and down the string, from the first to second to fourth fret, she missed the note. Something that frustrated Sullivan more than it should.

"Stop moving your finger up the string," he said.

"Sorry?" said the girl, pausing.

"You're making the tune sound all... staccato. And wrong. Use all four fingers."

"But it hurts."

"It does, at first."

Sullivan sat next to her, showing her the ends of his fingers. Each one was rough and flattened by a neat slab of dead skin.

"I haven't touched a string in years, but guitar fingers don't go. Eventually, the ends of your fingers become rough and used to it."

"But I don't want my fingers to become rough."

"Just the ends. And why wouldn't you? It shows you play guitar. No one can ever disrespect someone who plays the guitar. Here, can I show you?"

She handed the guitar to him, and he placed it across his knee. The shape was familiar, like the hand of an old friend on his back, or a song that he hadn't heard since he was a kid.

He placed a finger on fret one, his middle finger on fret two, his third finger on fret three, and his little finger on fret four. He plucked each of the first four frets on the E string, did the same with A, and the rest.

He did this once, slowly, then again, quickly.

"Wow, how d'you do that so fast?" Cassy asked.

"Practice. Do this exercise every day for ten minutes. Within weeks you'll find your fingers able to move up the string in ways you only dreamed about."

He played a quick tune to demonstrate, his fingers moving all over the place. Then he handed the guitar back.

She placed her four fingers on the string just as he had and played the four frets on E, continued on A, and moved onto the other strings. She tried this a few times, going a little quicker with each attempt.

"Now try playing what you were playing, but with all your fingers."

She did. She played *Twinkle Twinkle*. The rhythm sound clearer, nothing like the disjointed attempt of minutes ago.

"See, how much better is that?" he said.

"Thanks!"

He forced a smile. He wasn't used to someone thanking him. It prompted a sickness in his gut.

"Do you have a guitar?" she asked.

"Nah. Used to."

"What did you have?"

"A Fender."

"A Fender!"

"Yeah. It was beautiful as well. Black finish, white around the strings, but not the cheap looking black and white — this guitar sparkled. It literally sparkled."

"Sounds awesome. Why did you get rid of it?"

He looked down. "I had to."

"Why?"

"Just did."

A moment of silence passed.

"Would you teach me more stuff?" she asked.

"More? I have to go."

"I don't mean now. I mean when you get back. Later. Or tomorrow. I don't mind."

He looked at the kid. Her enthusiasm, her tenacity — it reminded him so much of Talia, and he wished he could teach her everything in the world.

"I'm not coming back."

"Why not?"

"I–"

"You're a lot nicer than the last guy Grandad had working

for him. He ran away, and we never saw him again. He left, too."

Sullivan considered this. What a disappointment he would be. Right now, he could be anything to this girl. A mentor, an inspiration, even a friend.

Sometimes things are best left a happy memory, rather than left to become a sad situation.

"Got the keys," said Connor.

Sullivan looked up at Connor, leant against the barn door. He realised that Connor must have been there for some time.

Sullivan followed Connor to the car.

Connor paused before he opened it.

Sullivan looked to him expectantly.

"You still think you have nothing to offer us?"

Sullivan rolled his eyes. "Open the car."

"Just hear me out."

"Open it or I'll just walk."

"Please, just — listen." Connor put his hands in the air, as if in a surrender motion.

Sullivan leant against the car and folded his arms.

"I need a guy," Connor said. "Someone who isn't scared of physical labour. For some money."

"I have money."

"A roof over their head then. Someone who can help me with the harvest. For a few weeks, that's all."

"What happened to the last guy?"

Connor sighed. "She told you, huh?"

"Told me what?"

"He disappeared. Just left, like that. I don't know. Nathaniel seemed skittish, like a troubled kid. I wanted to help him, but some people just don't want to be helped."

"And you think I want to be helped?"

Connor shook his head. "No, of course not. I don't see anyone ever helping you."

"Then what do you–"

"It's us that need the help."

"I'm not going to be your granddaughter's new–"

"Guitar teacher? All she's had so far is YouTube tutorials. She would benefit from an actual lesson or two."

Sullivan turned. Leant against the car. Stretched his arms. Growled.

"You don't know me," he said.

"That's fine. You don't want us to know who you are, what your name is, that's fine."

"I don't want you to get hurt."

Connor stepped forward. Put a hand on Sullivan's back.

"It's a few weeks. Help with the harvest. I'm getting too old for this, and Cassy is still too young. Where else am I supposed to find someone?"

"That why you picked me up? For labour?"

"I picked you up because I thought you might appreciate not being beaten up. Why you were so drunk is not for me to question. But maybe we–"

"Stop."

Sullivan stretched his back. Looked at the farm. Countryside in its most glorious form. The middle of nowhere.

Cassy sat in the open doors of the barn, plucking away at the guitar strings.

Elsie inside, water for a cup of tea on the stove and beers in the fridge.

"Fine," Sullivan grunted. "But I sleep in the barn."

"Really, we have a room inside for you that–"

"No. Barn. That will be where I sleep. I am not imposing myself on your family."

And I need to be outside so I can see any threats.

"As you wish."

Connor offered his hand. Sullivan shook it.

He wondered how much he would come to regret doing so.

CHAPTER EIGHT

FOR THE NEXT FEW DAYS, SULLIVAN KEPT HIS HEAD DOWN, kept busy, and said little to anyone.

He and Connor would rise at the first sign of light, often up before the roosters and only just beating the sun. It didn't take much for Connor to teach Sullivan what he needed to do — not only was Sullivan a fast learner, he despised being given instructions. Connor was not at all patronising, but Sullivan disliked being told how to perform menial tasks, so he waved Connor away as soon as he had the hang of it.

And so, until Elsie called them in for lunch, they would spend their mornings out in the fields, with Cassy playing around them. One day Cassy cycled around the field, the other she was playing with the dog, and another she was kicking a ball into a net, then fetching it out and kicking it in again.

She was always alone. Sullivan wasn't sure whether it was by choice. She didn't, however, seem at all sad about it. And, wherever she went, she had that guitar in its case, over her back, like it was the closest thing she had to something of her own to care for.

Sometimes she would smile, or make a joke, or stare

absently with a smile of contentedness upon her face, and it would prompt a vague memory of Sullivan's daughter that he'd suppress to his unconscious.

As a child, Talia had been so much like her mother; who was murdered when Talia was just a baby.

She had grown into young girl who was tenacious, cheeky and smart. All qualities that Cassy seemed to possess.

Sullivan distracted himself from the thought by working harder.

Occasionally, Connor spoke. "You want a break?" he sometimes asked, or, "You doing okay over there?" or, "Cassy not bothering you, is she?"

Each time, Sullivan batted the question away. A grunt or the wave of his hand and he would take a swig from his bottle of water, then return to his labour.

He did exactly as Connor showed him. He would look to see if the plant's tassels had turned. If they had, he'd squeeze the kernels between his fingers to check they were ready. Once a milky fluid was released, he would determine that the piece of corn was ready, and he would twist the corn away from its stalk. Later on, Elsie would use Cassy to help wrap each piece of corn and store them in fridges.

The repetitive motion was good.

It created a routine.

For someone who had never had a routine, it was nice to experience it. This was something resembling a normal life. The kind of work he'd never had to do and never needed to.

It comforted him that he found reward in hard work, despite his mass of money and the high number of deaths he had caused. What's more, the lack of alcohol and the labour was making him feel better. He felt fitter, more like he did back in his prime.

After a few days, on a sunny midday, Sullivan carried the last of the crops into the house and walked upstairs to wash his hands. As he did, the open door from the room furthest down the corridor distracted him. There was something in it that intrigued him...

He opened the door, revealing a small office; or, at least, something resembling an office. A small desk with a book cupboard beside it filled most of its space.

But there, against the wall, it stood.

An electric guitar.

Not just any electric guitar, however.

A Gibson.

And not just any Gibson – a 1960 Les Paul Gibson.

This was a guitar worth thousands. It had a tangerine body, curved like a big circle over a smaller circle. It was a thing of beauty.

It was, however, a wreck.

The main space of its body had a large crack. The fret board was hung backwards. The pegs were loose, and two were missing. The strings were broken. The knobs were missing.

How had something of such magnificence been left to such neglect?

"Are you admiring my Gibson?" came Connor's voice from behind him.

Sullivan turned, about to explain himself, but the smile on Connor's face was friendly and approachable.

"1960, isn't it? Les Paul?" Sullivan said.

"You know your guitars."

"My father had one similar. I think it was a 58."

"Oh, yeah? He let you play on it much?"

Sullivan scoffed. He was lucky if his father cared enough to feed him, never mind teach him guitar.

"Not when he was looking," Sullivan admitted.

"How could you not let a son play such an instrument?" Connor walked in, picked up the guitar, rotated it, and handed it to Sullivan. "Why don't you have a go?"

Sullivan was proud to lift the model, but it was hardly playable.

"It only has two working strings," he said.

"You are correct. Sadly so. I was planning on giving this to Cassy when she turned twelve and started guitar lessons at her school. Unfortunately, I'm not sure where to even start in repairing it."

Sullivan placed the guitar across his chest. Held it like he was playing it. Suddenly, he was fourteen years old again, hoping his dad would be too drunk to make it home, sneaking into his bedroom just to hold it. He never dared play it, but he would just hold it. And pretend.

Like a whole crowd of paying fans were ready to watch him play.

Like an adoring public was waiting for his excellent performance.

It was a Jay Sullivan he didn't recognise anymore. Did he really used to have such dreams?

Hell, he ended up in a job where he travelled the world. Earned lots of money. What could be better?

Perhaps a job where your employers don't turn on you. A job where you don't lose your wife and daughter. A job where you don't end up a loner alcoholic.

Connor put a hand on Sullivan's shoulder and smiled.

Sullivan flinched at the touch of the hand. Was his anguish really that obvious?

"Why don't you hang onto it for now?" Connor suggested. "See what you can do with it."

"But I couldn't take it."

"I didn't say take it. Hang onto it." Connor winked. "It's time for lunch."

What a strange action a wink is. It can mean so many things, and Sullivan was never sure how to interpret it from another man — what with it being an action he would normally use to precede fucking.

But he liked it.

It made him feel wanted.

And, for a minute, he forgot how wrong it was for him to feel that.

CHAPTER NINE

SULLIVAN LAY THE GUITAR ON A WOODEN CHEST LEFT IN THE barn, beside the old, single bed Connor had brought out for him. He sat on the bed and studied it.

He'd ask Connor to get some strings when he next drove into town. Possibly pick him up some wood, if they didn't have any lying around.

He'd repair the old, battered, broken body, and give it a new paint finish. Talia used to paint when she was nine. How hard could it be?

"Hey," came a child's voice.

Sullivan covered the guitar with a cloth and turned to Cassy, who stood in the doorway. He had been reluctant to keep engaging with her for fear of her becoming attached. Kids don't understand why someone has to leave, or why a man is a bad man. How would he explain to Cassy why he eventually had to leave if he kept tutoring her on the guitar?

"Hi," he replied.

"Can I show you something?"

He sighed. He wanted to say no, but he couldn't bring himself to, so she took his silence as a yes.

"Look," she said, and placed her fingers on the frets of her guitar. She did the exercise where she played a finger on each fret, just as he'd taught her. Only now, she was doing it quicker, and far more smoothly.

"Impressive," Sullivan said, trying not to engage with her, but unable to stop himself from being pleased with her progress.

"Now listen," she said, and played *Twinkle Twinkle*.

She was brilliant.

She played it with tempo, with quick fingers. She even added a jazzy twang by bending the string on one of the notes.

"Well done!" Sullivan said. He clapped; he couldn't help it. He knew he shouldn't grow to like this girl, but there was something so endearing about her. Something that made you want her to do well.

"What song should I learn next?" she asked.

Sullivan pulled a face, pretending to think.

"Ooh, I don't know. What's your favourite songs? Any more nursery rhymes?"

"I found a tab on the internet for the opening riff to *Sweet Child of Mine!*"

"Perfect!"

Sullivan stuck out his bottom lip. He was impressed by her song choice; Connor must have had some influence.

"Shall I go get it now? You could help."

"Maybe... maybe later."

She turned to go, then stopped. Turned back.

"I'm glad you're here," she said.

"Me too, Talia."

He smiled.

She stared at him.

He wondered why she was staring at him.

Then she said it.

"Who's Talia?"

Talia?

How the hell did she know about Talia?

Shit.

He realised.

He'd just called her Talia.

What the fuck was wrong with him?

This girl wasn't Talia.

He shouldn't think she is.

Remember what happened to Talia...

Cassy had her whole life ahead of her. She didn't need him coming along and fucking it up. She didn't need some deadbeat has-been causing irreparable damage.

What was he doing?

"Who's Talia?" Cassy repeated.

"Please leave," Sullivan said.

"But I just want to—"

"*Go!*"

Sullivan was panting.

His voice echoed around the barn.

His fingernails dug into his palm. His teeth grinded. His heart screamed for pills. But none of that was as painful as the look on Cassy's face as her eyes widened, and she looked afraid of him. A brief glimmer of fear before she ran away.

"No, wait, I didn't—"

But she was gone.

He put his hands on his face.

Refused to weep.

He was Jay fucking Sullivan. He didn't weep.

So, instead, he stood. Took hold of the edge of the bed and turned it over with a roar. Kicked a nearby troth so hard it his toe throbbed. Punched the wooden box the guitar stood on, forcing the guitar to slide into the straw below.

He screamed.

He screamed again.

Who was he?

Who the fuck was he?

So much for redemption.

There was no forgiveness. No way to undo a lifetime of killing.

There was only pain, and lots of it, in the wake of his every step.

He fell to his knees again.

And he didn't cry.

He just closed his eyes and waited for the anger to pass.

CHAPTER TEN

Sullivan craved beer. Or whiskey. Or whatever the hell he was able to get his hands on.

Luckily for him, Connor didn't question Sullivan's request. In fact, Connor was happy to oblige. He was heading into town that afternoon, and he was content to pick up some whiskey for him.

Sullivan tried to give him cash, asking him to get him the most expensive whiskey; if he was going to waste away his liver, he may as well do it in style. Connor, however, insisted it would be his pleasure. Sullivan could hardly tell Connor that he had millions and Connor did not, and he should just let Sullivan pay for it, so he had no choice but to accept the favour.

And so, that afternoon, they left Sullivan alone at the farm. Connor made his way to the store, and Elsie took Cassy to some kid's party.

Cassy hadn't wanted to go, as she was engrossed in some cartoon on the television. Eventually, she gave in. But she insisted on saying goodbye to Sullivan first. She ran up to him, spread her arms around his waist and gave him a hug.

He looked uncomfortably to Elsie, expecting Elsie to take her off.

Elsie did not. She just smiled warmly.

Sullivan awkwardly stroked Cassy's hair, looking around as if something in the room would save him.

"I like having you around," she said.

"Thanks," he reluctantly answered. "Er... me... too..."

And she left.

Sullivan searched the cupboards for what booze there was. A dusty bottle of sherry sat alone on a shelf. It would do.

He found a tumbler glass and poured the sherry.

He could hear the television coming from the living room. Cassy must have left it on. Dramatic music signalled the beginning of the news.

He hated the news.

He would keep up with it from time to time, such was the necessity of being on the run. But he was tired of hearing negative reports. Mostly, he was fed up of hearing news stories and knowing what was really behind them. The news anchors would report on suicides or tragic accidents, and he'd know the real reason behind the death.

He walked into the living room. Reached to switch the television off.

But the face that filled the screen caught his attention.

It took him a moment to realise it, but he recognised that man.

He was another Falcon. Another assassin that had worked for the government. His name was Grant. Sullivan had trained with him. The Falcons had entered them into the training program at the same time. They had both been eighteen. The Falcons had brainwashed them both into a life that eventually became so normal.

Many years ago, Sullivan and his wife had joined Grant and his wife, Stacey, for game nights. It was a regular Thursday tradition. Together, he and Grant had supported each other with the lies they had to give their families. It was part of their contract that loved ones could not know who they worked for, and they told their wives they worked for a business that sent them travelling around the world.

The lie was for their family's protection.

Of course, the game nights did not carry on after Sullivan's wife was murdered.

So much for the protection the lie provided.

He turned the volume up.

"This is Grant Dawson, a husband and father of three, and the suspected murderer of a politician and his eleven-year-old son. His body was discovered having shot himself last night following a turbulent few weeks."

"Oh, Grant..."

"A parent whose children share a school with Grant Dawson's son told us how, in the weeks leading to his death, Grant Dawson had arrived at the school gates with unexplained injuries, even once appearing with his arms bleeding. Eye witnesses also reported him causing a scene in a local supermarket. It remains unknown what caused this sudden change in behaviour."

Sullivan turned the television off.

He couldn't take anymore.

This wasn't the Grant he remembered. This was someone else.

The Grant he knew was generous. Caring. A wonderful father. A loving husband. A vibrant man, full of laughter. He would not do any of those things.

Was it possible that Grant's life as an assassin had caused him so much trauma? Was it killing a politician's child that had left him consumed with guilt? Had that caused this mental decline?

Sullivan was inclined not to believe that his trauma would have such effects, until he thought... *look at me.*

Would Grant recognise the person stood in his shoes today?

His thoughts led to Stacey. The kindest woman he knew.

He considered calling her.

He even picked up the phone, ready to dial.

But what would he say?

An explanation, perhaps. Something about who he was and what he and Grant did.

In working for the Falcons, each assassin would have to sign a document that stated what would happen following their death, and what their families would be told. Loved ones were permitted to know the truth once they were dead — or, at least, as little of the truth as the Falcons were willing to tell them. Both he and Grant agreed they wanted their loved ones to know they worked for the government — even if Grant was the only one out of the two of them with a loved one left to tell. They had also stipulated that, just as they had wanted the Falcons to explain the necessity of their deception, the last thing either of them had wanted was for their wives to think of them as liars. As a result, they had each left a video recording, approved by the Falcons, that would explain their actions in their own words.

Yet, despite Stacey now knowing the truth, she probably still didn't know what to think. Grant's final months must have seemed like a descent into madness, and the media were portraying Grant to be a dangerous man. Her image of him was open to manipulation.

The last thing Sullivan wanted was for Stacey to think Grant was a monster. They were working for the good guys.

Weren't we?

Even if Sullivan wasn't sure anymore, he just couldn't bear Stacey holding a tarnished memory of the man she loved, and a man that was such a dear friend to him. He had to speak to her.

But then what?

Would it change anything?

Would she listen?

He put the phone back.

Who was he kidding? He wasn't going to call. He wasn't a man who proactively helped people.

Instead, he would drink.

Ruminate.

Push all the dreadful memories to the back of his mind with as much alcohol as his body could handle.

It was what he was good at.

CHAPTER ELEVEN

A HIDDEN SNEER OF DISGUST FLICKERED ACROSS THE CORNERS of Charlene's mouth.

She stood in black, as was tradition. It seemed, as mother of the deceased, it was important that she painted herself head to toe in the most deathly, darkest image possible. Her long, black dress fell over her hefty bust and glided past her ankles. Her shoes propped her curvy legs up on thick heels. A netted veil dropped over her face, concealing grief from a face that normally held such beauty.

It was melodramatic, sure, but it was the only way she was able to hide the look of hatred she aimed at her husband.

And there he stood. The man of the hour. The glorious host.

Hugo Jones.

Charlene's supposed better half.

Married at twenty. Fucked around since twenty-one.

Stood in his expensive black pin-stripe suit, shaking hands with mourners who didn't seem to know this funeral would not be taking place if it weren't for him. But it didn't matter, he played the welcoming host, the saddened father, and his guests wouldn't dare say a thing against him.

He cared so much about appearances, and that was her purpose. She was his trophy. He took pride in having a beautiful woman on his arm, but that was the extent of his emotional investment. It was his ego that meant no man could ever touch her, not his love.

He had so many faces, she wasn't even sure which was the real Hugo. On day one she had met his handsome, warm face. The endearing face. The face that made you wonder why he had such a monstrous reputation.

And there was his face of power.

His face of aggression.

The face Charlene cowered from, silently, so the children wouldn't hear.

Had he shown that face to Nathaniel?

Just before Hugo took their son's life, had he shown his aggressive, powerful face?

The poor boy must have been so scared. He must have known what his father was about to do. He knew enough about who his father was.

He was seventeen. Not old enough to vote, but old enough to be accused of betrayal.

Hugo hadn't even bothered to hide it from her. He came home and gave her the news. Watched her break down and waited until she was done to ask when dinner would be ready.

Now he stood beside her as the coffin lowered into the ground. Displaying his face of despair. His face of anguish.

How could this have happened?

Simple.

It happened because of *you,* dear husband.

Everything bad that happens is because of *you.*

Hugo flexed his fingers and placed them around Charlene's.

He pretended that he was trying not to cry and, to everyone else, it may have even been convincing.

Not to her.

Anyone who accused her of being weak for allowing her husband to hold her hand after killing her son did not understand who or what her husband was.

No, she wasn't weak. She was strong; stronger than she'd ever been.

Because she withstood it.

She was still standing there. Alive. She wasn't broken, she hadn't allowed him to destroy her. She had used all of her strength to endure him.

This was not a marriage. It was a life sentence. And she was strong enough to overcome all those lonely nights in her cell.

But the time was coming where she would not endure any longer.

She was looking for an opportunity.

The death of her son was the final action he would take against her.

And she swore he would regret it.

CHAPTER TWELVE

Sitting on the porch, drinking his beer, Sullivan looked up at the night sky. At the stars. Thinking about all the worlds that were undiscovered. There could be trillions. Life must have evolved on some of them.

And that just proved it — how insignificant he was. How little this life mattered.

And, in a way, that comforted him.

To be aware that, no matter what he did, it meant nothing. It barely caused a ripple in time. This world existed for billions of years without him and would carry on for billions more just the same.

"Mind if I join you?" Connor asked, sitting next to Sullivan with a beer in hand.

Connor sat. They said nothing. Rested in comfortable silence.

"How is the barn treating you?" Connor finally said.

"Just fine."

"I would insist that there's no need for you to sleep there, and that we have a perfectly comfortable bedroom inside, but I imagine you'd just say the same thing."

"Yep."

"Do you have family?"

Sullivan looked down at his drink. What a question.

Did he have a family?

He had a daughter who was out there somewhere. Finding a way in the world without him. Causing him pain from afar.

He didn't want to talk about her.

Nor did he want to mention his deceased wife.

So he said nothing.

"It's complicated, right?" Connor said.

"Could say that."

"It so often is. I see other families, I see the way they dread their Christmases together, I see the way they fight and fall out, and I just think... gosh, I'm lucky."

Sullivan looked at Connor. He was intrigued.

"You see, even though I lost my daughter before I should have, and although no man should ever bury his child — we loved each other. There were rarely arguments. Of course, that doesn't include when she was a teenager. She rebelled pretty fiercely. But after that..."

Connor smiled. His face seemed to light up whenever he talked about his family.

"I consider myself a very lucky man, you know?"

"I know."

And so a tradition of sharing a beer in the evening began, and continued for the next few days. Sullivan rarely offered much to the conversation, but that didn't bother Connor. Connor would either fill the silence with his ramblings, or would allow the silence to sit there, comfortably.

Connor rarely asked questions.

That was why Sullivan enjoyed his company.

Connor did not ask any more about Sullivan's family. His past. Where he'd come from, where he was going. He never expected there to be much said from Sullivan.

And that bothered neither of them.

And, once it reached eleven and Connor declared it was time for bed, Sullivan would go back to the barn.

One day, however, Sullivan asked a question, after one of Connor's declarations surprised him.

"It's almost thirty years to the day since I bought this farm," Connor said.

"You bought it? I thought you inherited it."

"Ah, that's what most people assume. And that's probably how most people become farmers. But not me. I was a prosecution lawyer."

"What?"

"Yes. And I did some high-profile cases, I tell you that. Earned a lot of money."

"Why did you stop?"

"Well, I would like to say that the lure of the farm life caught me, but it wasn't like that. I was a city man. We raised our daughter in a flat in London that probably cost more than this whole farm. No, it was a case I had. I still think about it a lot these days."

"What was the case?"

Connor hesitated. Took a deep breath.

After all his ramblings, his comfortable talk, his endless conversation, this was the first time Sullivan had noticed him struggling with his words. Something in his eyes changed, faded, his humour shifting to melancholy.

"It was about the death of a child. Murdered by a stranger in their home. The police had enough evidence to pin it on this man but didn't want to bring charges. I couldn't understand why. So, I tried to do it myself. To prosecute without support. I would not let this murderer get away with it, and I didn't understand why the police would."

Connor paused. A grave stare in his eyes.

"But I do now."

He held his beer bottle to his lips and took a long gulp before continuing.

"I was told by a government official not to prosecute. They even offered me money for my lack of action. I didn't take it."

He stared at the beer bottle. Not sipping, just rotating it in his hand.

"When I refused the money, they offered me threats. In fear for my young family getting hurt, I had to drop it. I believe it was a sanctioned killing, by secret service or something. But what always bugged me about that idea was... why a child? Why would any government secret service authorise the killing of a child?"

"Were the parents killed too?"

"Oh, yes, they were murdered."

Sullivan wanted to answer Connor's question. He wanted to say; the child was most likely a mistake. The father was probably the target, and the child was a witness. The assassin had no choice.

But he no longer agreed with that anymore. There was always a choice, so long as you believed there was.

"I had to stop. I questioned everything. My job. Those in charge. The way society worked. And I decided I'd rather keep to myself, somewhere where I don't have to deal with a world I don't agree with. The following month, me and Elsie bought a farm. And we've had the best life we could dream of."

Connor gave a smile that was anything but genuine and continued to sip on his beer.

They said nothing else for the rest of that evening.

The following evening, Sullivan did not sit on the porch.

In fact, he did not sit on the porch again the next evening. Or the evening after that.

That story was the end of any kind of friendship that may

have begun. From then on, Sullivan assumed the role of worker, and continued to do a good job.

Connor didn't seem to question it, though Sullivan knew he wanted to.

CHAPTER THIRTEEN

THE ROOF OF THE BARN SPUN THE WAY IT DID MOST NIGHTS. Leaks dripping upon his drunken face. Nausea was now as normal to Sullivan as his feeling of guilt, or idiocy, or the knowledge that the world would be so much better off without him.

What's this world with one less killer?

A part of him wanted to believe it wasn't as simple as that. The other part of him insisted that the world wouldn't see it that way.

If everyone knew the truth of who he was and what he'd done, would they see him as the same as any other serial killer?

Many people might still be alive if he had not been involved.

Then again, maybe they wouldn't. Should he have not been around to execute the hit, there would probably have been another assassin ready to do it instead.

He was sixteen when his father murdered Sullivan's mother and turned the gun on himself. Until then, his childhood had been nothing but beatings and abuse.

He'd entered the system. Fought anyone who looked at him the wrong way. Confronted anyone who dared say something bad about him.

In retrospect, it made sense why they recruited him two years later. He'd grown up being used to violence. He was already numb to the sight. He was a damaged orphan, ready to be conditioned into their puppet.

His conscience initially told him killing was wrong. But they had methods to silence that conscience.

They told him he had a purpose. Channelled his rage into combat training. That was probably why he was so good — anger fuelled him, and he had a lot of it.

Then came the day of his first kill.

They made it easy, of course. Sullivan hadn't had to track anyone; they had done that for him. All he had to do was pull the trigger.

The man was tied to a chair. Crying. Sullivan's mentor, a guy named Alexander, told Sullivan to shoot.

Sullivan said no.

Everything in his body screamed no.

They had taught him to do this, but somehow, he couldn't.

Alexander took him outside.

Sat him down.

Showed him a newspaper headline.

A picture of this man filled the front page, looking healthier and less sweaty. The headline read:

PAEDOPHILE KILLS FIFTH GIRL.

"Once," Alexander told him, "I was where you are now. They gave me a gun, told me to point and shoot. And I said no. Just like you."

"Really?" Sullivan said, his voice so young, so full of hope.

"That guy escaped. You know what happened?"

"What?"

"He killed a further three girls. Raped them too. And I could have stopped him. But I didn't. Because I was a coward."

Sullivan looked to his feet. Nodded.

"Look at this newspaper headline," Alexander said, thrusting it into Sullivan's vision. "Look at what he's done."

Sullivan gazed upon the article. This man was evil, no doubt about it. He deserved it.

"It won't always be like this, though, Jay," Alexander continued. "You will get a target and you won't know why they deserve to die, but they will. They will be evil, just like this man, and just like the man I let go. You must take it on faith that we will give you targets for the greater good."

Sullivan nodded. He was starting to understand.

"And that guy in there — you want him to kill anymore girls? You want him to rape anymore? What if that was a girl you knew? You cared about?"

Sullivan shook his head.

"Stop being a prissy little fool. Be a man. Go in there and do what your job demands you to do."

Sullivan took the gun. Walked absently back into the room. Looked at the man.

The man pleaded.

He didn't seem so scary.

"Don't let him fool you," Alexander said from behind Sullivan. "Don't let him convince you he is anything but what he is."

Sullivan aimed the gun, just as they had taught him.

He hated guns.

If he would do this then, from now on, he would do it without guns.

"Do it."

Sullivan held his breath.

He let a tear run down his cheek, knowing Alexander wouldn't see it.

"I'm waiting."

Sullivan kept hold of his breath.

Aimed.

Ignored the pleas.

Pulled the trigger.

He turned away. Closed his eyes and no longer disguised his crying.

Alexander grabbed Sullivan's chin and turned his head.

"Open your eyes."

Sullivan refused.

"Open them!"

Sullivan opened his eyes.

There was a man. Bullet hole in his head. Body slumped.

Because of him.

He dropped the gun.

"Good," Alexander said. "You did the right thing. Many lives have been saved because of you. Now sit down."

Sullivan sat down.

A group of men took the corpse away.

Five minutes later, they brought another man in, kicking and screaming, and placed in the chair. Tied. Bound. Pleading.

Alexander picked up the gun and gave it to Sullivan.

"Another?" Sullivan said.

"Yes. And another, and another, until you stop crying and do it."

Sullivan looked into the prisoner's eyes. They were just the same as the previous man's eyes. Desperate. Distraught. Knowing everything was about to end.

"What did this guy do?" Sullivan asked.

Alexander shook his head. "I'm not saying."

"What?"

"Just like I told you. You won't always get to know. We give you a target and a job to do. So do it."

"I can't do it without knowing–"

"Yes, you can. Be a man, Sullivan. You know what to do."

Sullivan looked to the gun. He dropped it.

"Pick up the gun," Alexander instructed.

"I don't want to use a gun."

Alexander sighed. Took a knife from its place beside his ankle. Handed it to Sullivan.

Sullivan looked it over.

Moved forward.

Held it out to this man's neck.

"Please…" the man begged. "I'm innocent."

More tears came, but Sullivan did it.

And they removed the corpse.

And they brought in another man.

Each time, Alexander told Sullivan that evil people deserved to die.

To take it on faith.

That Sullivan was doing the right thing.

He was serving his country, and the country owed him.

Eventually, Sullivan stopped crying.

He stopped questioning.

He killed them quicker.

And Alexander decided it was time that they ventured out into the real world and did this, his parting words repeating around Sullivan's head like a bad echo: "We recruited you because you think you have nothing to offer — but you do. You see, Sullivan, death is a pivotal part of life, and that is what you offer the world. *Death*."

And, as Sullivan lay in the barn, thinking back to this pivotal point of his life, he wondered what he might have done differently.

His thoughts drifted to Stacey.
What she must think of Grant...
He needed to tell her the truth.
He needed her to know.

CHAPTER FOURTEEN

THE NEXT EVENING, AS CONNOR PUSHED CASSY ON THE swings and Elsie sipped on a glass of wine in the garden, Sullivan found his way upstairs to the phone.

It had been a while since he had dialled this number, but he still knew it.

Funny, really, how the memory holds onto things like that. As if the useless information he retained would someday be useful.

The phone rang.

Dread overcame Sullivan. He couldn't bear Stacey thinking that Grant was some kind of monster, she had to know the truth.

He thought about what he would say, considered further the implications of what he would tell Stacey, how she'd react, or how he'd even begin talking — then she answered the phone, and he had to stop panicking.

"Hello?"

"Hi, er... is that — is that Stacey?"

"Yes. Who is this?"

"It's... Jay Sullivan."

Silence on Stacey's end made Sullivan think this probably hadn't been the best idea, and he considered hanging up.

Then she spoke, and he heard the effects of the last few weeks in her voice.

"Oh, Jay... Thank God..."

"It's been a while."

"It's been a long while. But I'm glad you called."

"I saw on the news what happened. I'm sorry."

"The news... The god damn news... They are camped out on my lawn, Jay. Every time I walk outside, or even just appear at the window, the cameras go off and they shout questions. They frighten my children in their own home."

"Don't worry about the reporters. They'll go once another bit of news arrives. How are you?"

An audible sigh was his response.

"I don't know, Jay."

"Look, I know I should have been in touch more, but the past few years have been rocky, and that's no excuse, but–"

"Don't worry. It's fine. I'm glad you're calling now. It's good to talk to someone who knew Grant before all this."

"That wasn't Grant. You believe that, right?"

"I don't even know anymore."

"Stacey, come on. He can't have been himself."

"But how do I know, Jay? We don't even know Grant. You won't believe this, but this whole time, he's been working for some kind of government... thing... and I never knew. He lied to both of us. How are we supposed to know who he is?"

"Listen, Stacey–"

"I mean, for God's sake, he was a murderer. He killed people for a living. What if he'd turned the gun on me?"

"He would never have done that."

"But how do you even know that, Jay?"

"Because I know."

"But how? Everything was a lie. His job. Our marriage. Our whole life."

"That wasn't a lie."

"How could that possibly be true?"

"Because I worked for them too."

Silence.

Sullivan waited for her to speak, but she didn't.

He waited and waited, trying not to imagine the thoughts racing through her mind.

"I am such a fool," she finally said.

"It's not simple, Stacey. They recruited us as teenagers. We had messed up childhoods, we didn't know any better, and they taught us that this was... He's not a murderer. It was a job."

"A job? It's still murder, whether it is a job or not."

"We were soldiers."

"Soldiers? Are you fucking kidding, Jay?"

"Stacey, please, calm down."

"My husband killed himself! Do not tell me to calm down. I am so *sick* of people telling me to calm down."

"I'm just trying to say it wasn't that simple. The employers turned on me, which is why I've been gone, and... Really, let me explain."

"Jay, I... All this time? All this time you have known? Both of you lying to me? Every evening we spent together, you and Grant sat there with your dirty little secret, and I had no idea."

"It was for your protection."

She snorted an ironic laugh.

"Don't call here again, Jay."

The line went dead.

Sullivan rested his head against the wall, listening to the dial tone.

Should he ring back?

Should he try to explain himself?

His better judgement told him not to, and, for once, he listened to it.

She called Grant a murderer.

But they were with the good guys.

Weren't they?

It was a job.

Sullivan slid down the wall, to the floor, and recalled that day with Alexander.

The way each murder grew easier and easier.

The way they kept bringing them in.

Sullivan decided he wasn't even sure he knew who the good guys were anymore — or if there even was such a thing.

It was time to leave this poor family alone.

It was time to disappear into obscurity once again.

It was what he deserved.

CHAPTER FIFTEEN

THE CORNFIELD WAS EMPTY, AND THE WORK WAS DONE. They planted more, but they would take sixty to eighty days until they were ready, providing conditions were correct. Sullivan did not plan to stay that much longer.

He was getting complacent. Falling into comfort. Creating a home for himself.

Complacency and comfort created the best conditions to be murdered. He would strike a target when they felt most at home, when they felt safe.

And he should never allow himself to feel safe.

He would not put this family in danger.

He spent his final evening like he'd spent all those before. With a toolbox, various materials, and a guitar in severe need of repair. Slowly, the guitar was resembling the thing of beauty it once was.

"Hey," came a voice from the door of the barn.

Sullivan turned. It was Connor.

"Sorry," said Connor. "I went to say your name, only I realised we still don't know it."

This was a clear prompt for Sullivan to finally reveal his name. He stood, remaining silent.

"Come," Connor said, and walked away.

Sullivan hesitated.

He didn't like being told to follow someone without a reason. He stared at the guitar, nearly finished. He'd carry on later. He followed Connor to the porch of the house where two wooden chairs awaited them. Connor sat on one, taking a bottle of beer for himself and holding one out for Sullivan.

"Come," Connor said. "Sit."

Sullivan looked at the chair reluctantly.

"This is my last night here," Sullivan said.

"I guessed as much," Connor replied. "In which case, let's have one final beer to mark the occasion."

Sullivan looked at the beer.

"I'm an old man. I don't get much company. Let me at least give you a beer as a thank you for all the hard work you've put in."

Sullivan took the beer and sat down.

He turned the beer bottle. It was a Scottish beer. One he didn't recognise.

He took a swig.

It was good.

He hadn't had as much alcohol as he was used to in the past few weeks. It had been good to be free of it. To have a body empty of poison. He'd felt sick at first, but now he felt more refreshed. More alive.

Only problem was, the more alive he felt, the more it hurt.

"Where do you think you'll go?" Connor asked.

Sullivan paused. He hadn't thought about it.

"Don't know," Sullivan replied, taking a large swig of beer.

"Don't suppose I can persuade you to stay a little longer?"

Sullivan shook his head.

"Cassy will miss you," said Connor.

"She'll be fine."

"Those guitar lessons you've been giving her have really paid off. I'd give her some lessons myself, but my fingers aren't what they used to be. But with you... She is going to better than Clapton and Hendrix in no time."

"Kid's got YouTube now. She can find some lessons on there."

"Ah, yes. YouTube. The death of us all. Isn't that right?"

Sullivan couldn't help but smile. "Got that right."

"I was wondering." Connor took a big, deep breath. "Course you don't have to tell me what's none of my business, but I was just wondering what makes you think you don't fit in here?"

Sullivan shook his head. This beer immediately felt like a mistake.

"I don't want to make you uncomfortable. I can see you don't say much, and you keep yourself to yourself. You insist on staying in that barn, God knows why, but that's up to you, I don't question it. But, honestly, you don't seem like a bad bloke. You may be quiet, but you've never been nasty. You work harder than any man I've ever employed. You are better with my granddaughter than anyone else who's stayed here. I was just wondering why you don't think you'd fit in here. I don't see you being a danger to us."

Sullivan twirled the beer bottle, reading the label but paying no attention to the words. He looked up at the late evening sky, savouring the warmth of a summer that won't last much longer.

"You know nothing about me, Connor," he said. "I've seen bad people that look good, and good people look bad. Don't trust so easily."

"I don't trust easily. But I trust you."

Sullivan took in a big breath, held it, and let it go. Just like one does when aiming a sniper rifle. Calm your breathing and exhale with the gun.

He hated guns.

He looked to Connor.

He knew how to use that beer bottle to choke him.

He knew how to smash that wooden chair and create a piece of splintered wood that could slice his neck.

He knew how to press his thumbs against the right part of the throat to kill him the quickest.

He didn't want to hurt anyone anymore.

He'd given up seeking redemption. Now he just wanted a quiet life; to live out the rest of his days somewhere he could be left alone to feel shit for the things he'd done.

"Would you like a lift in the morning?" Connor asked. "If you still insist in going, that is."

"No. You've done enough. I'll walk."

"It's easily four or five miles until the next village."

"I'm used to long walks. I'll be fine."

"Well, if this is the last evening we are together, I would like to say thank you." Connor raised his beer. "To you, Mr Whoever-You-Are. The finest helping hand and guitar tutor I ever had at this farm."

Sullivan nodded uncomfortably. He drank the rest of his beer.

He stood.

Placed the empty beer bottle beside the chair.

Nodded at Connor.

"Thank you," he said.

He paused, waiting to say more.

But nothing else came out of his mouth.

Just stutters and silence.

He turned and walked away, returning to his bed in the barn.

BEIRUT, LEBANON

CHAPTER SIXTEEN

IT WAS ONCE A CITY OF BEAUTY, BUT THAT BEAUTY HAD SINCE been destroyed. The civil war may have ended in 1990, but the recovery was still ongoing. The Syrian occupation had only just ended. The assassination of the prime minister was official.

This should have inspired hope, but many were still defiant. People were still contesting who exactly was behind the explosion that had killed Rafic Hariri.

Countries in the West claimed they were not interfering in any war with Syria. That was the official statement.

Sajid Ahmed knew it was untrue, just as he knew having such knowledge made him a target. He knew the danger he was in. And he knew he was being chased.

The man in the car behind him wore a facial disguise, but that was probably more to protect him from debris than to conceal his identity.

Jay Sullivan didn't care if Sajid saw his identity.

Jay Sullivan was untouchable.

He didn't need to hide his face. His face incited fear. People saw it and knew they would not survive.

Sajid looked to Aqeel in the seat beside him. He didn't care about his life, he just had to get his son somewhere safe. Sullivan could do whatever with him.

With Sullivan on his tail, Sajid could now be sure that this had extended beyond the politics of his country. The west was interfering, despite every declaration to the contrary. This man would not be chasing him otherwise.

The car came up behind Sajid's.

Too close. Almost touching.

Sajid couldn't go anywhere. He couldn't drive quicker for fear he'd crash.

He tried to turn. As he did, Sullivan poked the nose of his car into Sajid's, and the vehicle span; slowly at first, then faster and faster, until it was completely out of control. Smoke from the airbags made him cough. The bangs of the wheels bursting told him there would be no escape.

When the car finally came to a stop and the airbag deflated, Sajid looked at his son. Bloody and mangled in the seat next to him.

His son's eyes widened, but Aqeel didn't even have chance to warn his father about the grenade soaring through the sky.

But he had a chance to see their killer.

To look at Sullivan's eyes from afar.

Then his car exploded, and his life was over.

Sullivan had thought nothing of that look. That expression on the boy's face. The desperate panic in the seconds where a young child realised his life was about to end.

But he thought about it now.

He knew it was just a memory fed into a dream. It was trauma punching its way through from his subconscious.

But that didn't make it any easier to watch.

It was his punishment, and he knew he deserved it.

He fought to open his eyes; begged his sub-conscious to end the torture.

As he woke up, returning to the barn, sweating, his eyes fell on the repaired guitar across from the bed.

His panting took a while to calm down.

And even though he stared at that guitar, all he saw was the boy's face.

That split-second glance that lasted forever in his mind.

He was burdening this family. They were housing a murderer. And he didn't deserve their affection.

It was time to leave.

FROME, ENGLAND

CHAPTER SEVENTEEN

WHEN EXECUTING A HIT, ONE DOESN'T JUST CHARGE IN AND kill everyone. It's not like it is in the movies. It's a lot more careful than that.

One watches. Learns. Observes.

Ensures one has the correct target.

Ensures that one is in the right place. That it is the right time. The right moment.

Amateurs rush in and leave a messy death. Professionals saunter in and leave chaotic beauty.

And that was exactly what Wayne, Simon, Raul and Damien were doing. They were waiting. Ensuring.

They'd followed the farmer to town every afternoon, watching him as he pulled up in his Volkswagen Sharan. Connor would step out, straighten his shirt as if it would disguise the smell of farm life, and walk into the hardware store.

It was always the hardware store, then the supermarket. Except for the one day when he went to the music store and came out with a pack of guitar strings.

That was the only day he had diverted from his routine.

At all other times, they stopped along the only road leading to Connor's farm. He lived far away from anyone else. Miles away, in fact.

This was both an advantage and a disadvantage.

The hit would be secluded. No witnesses. No onlookers.

But it also made it obvious when they were staking the house out.

They only drove close enough to see the house once, then stayed far back, keeping their distance.

There had counted four people at the farm.

The farmer, Connor.

His wife, Elsie. The second target.

The granddaughter. The third.

And some other guy. A recent addition. A guy who appeared to be a helping hand, someone Connor was probably paying to help with the harvest.

But he was also a potential witness.

They could kill him too. But it wasn't sensible. They had their targets, and Hugo would have gone to great lengths to ensure that no one would attribute the death of these targets to them. If they added a body that Hugo wasn't expecting, then who knows what it would do to his plans.

And you *do not* mess with Hugo's plans.

So they waited.

The harvest was nearly over. Their cornfield was almost empty. Which meant the farmer wouldn't need a helping hand any more.

Which meant this guy would no longer have a purpose to stay.

Which meant that, surely, he would soon be leaving.

If the guy didn't go, they'd contact Hugo. But that was the extreme circumstance. They still had a week to fulfil the contract. They could wait.

But the harvest was done, and they knew the man had no purpose for being there.

They parked along the country road leading to the farm and waited. Readied their weapons.

As soon as the man walked past, they would drive up to the house and execute the hit.

It shouldn't be long.

CHAPTER EIGHTEEN

Cassy was waiting on the porch with Connor and Elsie stood behind her.

Sullivan trudged over to her, holding the guitar.

You wouldn't have been able to tell this guitar had ever been damaged. Its body was clean and robust. Its strings had been restrung and retuned. Its fret board replaced and attached.

"Do you know what this is?" Sullivan asked her.

She shook her head but was unable to contain her excitement. She stared at it, mouth agape.

"This was your father's Gibson. It's worth thousands — if you consider its worth in money, that is. Really, it's priceless."

"Wow..."

He handed it to her.

"For me?" she asked.

"Well, it was your grandfather's. But, since I repaired it, I was hoping he'd allow me to pass it on to you."

"The thing would be wasted on me," Connor said. "Of course."

She took the guitar and held it. Did not play it, did not

twirl it, did not even touch the strings — just held it. Staring at it. Marvelling at it.

"Thank you!" she said.

Sullivan smiled awkwardly. He wasn't sure how to handle gratitude from children. Usually they looked at him in terror because he'd just murdered their parents, not because he'd done something genuinely nice for them.

"I have something for you too," Cassy said. She handed Connor the guitar to hold and ran back inside.

"You sure we can't give you a lift?" Connor asked.

"No, I'll be fine."

"Or stay for lunch?" Elsie asked.

"Really, I should be on my way."

"Why?" asked Connor.

"Excuse me?"

"I mean, I just wish I knew what it is about you that's such a secret. You've done all this and you're still going to leave without us even knowing your name."

Cassy returned from the house with a piece of paper. She handed it to Sullivan.

On it was a poorly drawn self-portrait of herself holding a guitar, scribbled with a brown crayon that didn't stay within the lines. Next to her was a man Sullivan assumed to be himself. Beneath the drawing was a message reading:

Thank you for the guitar lessons. You're the best teacher I've ever had.
Cassy x x x x

Sullivan's eyes flickered. Tears formed.

But he would let no one see such a thing.

He just looked at Cassy, smiling through the sadness.

"Thank you," he said.

He folded the piece of paper and placed it inside his pocket.

No one had done anything this nice for him in a long time.

No one since...

He closed his eyes and forced thoughts of Talia away.

He looked to Connor, who smiled back at him; though it was not a smile of happiness.

Sullivan went to thank Connor and Elsie, but he didn't know how. He was not good at expressing gratitude. It wasn't something he'd ever really tried.

He decided he'd do the next best thing.

"My name is Jay," he said. "Jay Sullivan."

Connor grinned. "Suits you."

"Sounds like some kind of action hero," said Elsie.

"Oh, I assure you," Sullivan said, "I am no hero."

He looked to Cassy, who was now plucking at a few strings on her new guitar.

He tried to speak again but didn't.

He nodded.

And he turned, walking away.

Not looking back.

Until, eventually, the family was gone, and he was alone on a country lane, walking between empty fields.

And, just like that, he left their lives as quickly as he'd entered them.

But something felt uncomfortable.

Not him leaving, nor him being there for as long as he did.

Something else.

Something in the pit of his stomach he could not shake.

A feeling that, by walking away, he left that family in danger.

Which was ridiculous. Paranoia. Post-traumatic stress, or something like it.

Death was all he had to offer the world, and it would be all he had to offer them.

So he walked on, telling himself to stop being so pathetic.

This was exactly why he had to leave.

Because, the longer you stay, the more you come to care. And Sullivan was not cruel enough to subject another person to what happens when he cares about them.

CHAPTER NINETEEN

IT WAS THE END OF SUMMER, AND THE SUN WAS LINGERING like a guest who'd stayed too long. Sullivan didn't mind the sun, but he loved the rain, and he was looking forward to when the weather wasn't making everyone so damn happy.

He traipsed down the country road, regretting not taking a bottle of water. He expected a stitch after walking a few miles, but it didn't come. The work in the field had evidently been good for him.

He had not seen a signpost for a while, but he assumed he was going in the right direction. This was the only road.

Then something startled him.

A car. Black. Expensive. Possibly a Bugatti.

A car that looked completely out of place.

This was a city car. A car that a man who was clearly compensating for something would drive around, revving the ridiculously loud engine and accelerating quickly at traffic lights.

It was odd to see one here. This road only led to one place: the farm.

Perhaps they were lost.

No...

A car like this doesn't get lost in a place like this...

He slowed down as he approached the car. He tried to see who was behind the wheel, but the windows were blacked-out.

He peered into the distance; the main road might be nearby, and they'd probably turned off to figure out where they were going.

He listened for the sound of traffic but heard nothing but birds and crickets.

He knocked on the window.

It wound down. A young man stared back. Possibly mid-twenties. Tattoos across his arms. A who-the-fuck-are-you expression on his face. Like he owned the world. Like no one should ever tell him what to do.

Three more men of similar appearance were in the car, but Sullivan struggled to see them. The blacked-out windows made it dark inside.

He could still tell, however, that every set of eyes were on him.

"Can I help you, amigo?" the man asked in a Birmingham accent. The word *amigo* seemed particularly out of place in his voice. He chewed with his mouth open, but Sullivan could see no gum.

"I was just wondering if you were lost?"

"Why?"

Sullivan looked around.

Without intentionally doing so, his mind scanned for weapons and ways he could use them.

Tree branch.

Car exhaust.

Big rock.

The man drummed his fingers on the wheel. His knuckles were tattooed. One read *fuck* while the other read *cunt*.

Delightful.

"Just seems an odd place for you to be, is all," Sullivan said.

"That so?"

"Was wondering what you might be doing here."

"None of your fucking business."

Sullivan looked down.

He had sworn he wouldn't kill anyone else.

This kid was irritating him, yes — but being angry wasn't an excuse to hurt anyone.

Not anymore.

But what if Sullivan just wounded the brat?

Just hurt him a little?

No. Sullivan wouldn't be able to stop there. He would punch, punch again, and just keep punching until there was nothing left to punch.

He didn't have the self-restraint.

"Do you need help to find your way?" Sullivan asked.

"I need you to leave me the fuck alone, mate," the man replied. A few sniggers came from behind him.

"It's just—"

"Fuck off or you're gonna get smoked, you get me?"

What infuriated Sullivan far more than this delinquent's rudeness, threats, or general appearance, was the way he was practically taking a shit over the English language.

Language was power. Words can manipulate you in and out of any situation. They told everyone a lot about who you were.

And these words were telling Sullivan that this kid was an imbecile.

"What you looking at?" the man prompted. "What you gonna do?"

Sullivan had a decision to make.

One he didn't wish to make, but knew he had to.

Hurt these men. Wound them. Show them how you talk to another human, and risk killing another person.

Or walk away.

He struggled to choose the latter. Not just because something in his gut told him everything about this situation was wrong, but because it was his instinct to defend his pride with violence. He wasn't used to people daring to speak to him like this.

Which was exactly why he needed to walk away.

Because he did not want to hurt anyone else.

Even these idiots.

But why were they here?

The man took a blade from his pocket, held it casually beside his head, dangling it, as if he was flaunting a fashion accessory.

Sullivan was not impressed.

He'd been threatened with many knives in his time. It was actually quite convenient. It was a weapon he could take and use on that person himself.

But not this time.

Whatever they were doing, they were in the middle of the country.

Sullivan did not doubt there was some kind of illegal activity going on here. Maybe a drug exchange, or disposal of incriminating items. Possibly getting rid of a body.

Whatever.

It wasn't up the Sullivan to do the law's job.

He walked on.

"That's what I thought," he heard the man say, and it took everything in his body to hold back, to stop himself from cutting that prick's throat with his own blade.

"Let's go get them!" he heard another voice shout.

The engine revved.

They drove on.

Away from Sullivan.

Toward the farm.

He stopped walking.

Let's go get them…

Who was *them*?

There were only three people you could get to down that road.

And, as the sound of the engine faded away, he realised he should have just killed them all.

He turned and, ignoring the pain in his side, sprinted back toward the farm as quickly as his aching legs would take him. It was miles, and it took him longer than it once would have.

Just as the farmhouse entered his vision, he saw the car again, as it was leaving.

He dived behind a bush to hide. Whatever they had done, they would not wish to leave any witnesses.

The car sped past him, along the country road.

He did not hide because he feared a fight — not at all. He was ready for a fight.

He hid because something told him that his priority was getting to this family quickly.

He had to see if they were still alive, and if he could save them.

CHAPTER TWENTY

SULLIVAN ALREADY KNEW WHAT HE WOULD FIND BEFORE HE entered the house.

But he still had to see it.

He still had to know.

Even though his instinct, which had never proven him wrong, told him he did not want to see what he would see.

He ran. Sprinted. Surged. Forced his legs forward, ignoring how much they ached, battling through the moments he almost toppled over and the moments he staggered.

He reached the house.

The door was left open.

"Connor?" he shouted, running through the hallway, into the living room.

Silence.

Connor did not saunter through with his knowing smile and steam rising off his cup of tea. Elsie was not putting the washing on the radiators and there were no sounds of Cassy playing outside.

"Elsie?" he tried, running into the kitchen, and through to the dining area, looking out into the garden.

"Ta – Cassy?" he said, not so much shouting anymore, but gasping.

Not Cassy.

Please, not Cassy.

He reached the stairs, feeling the weight of the wood sink beneath each jump.

He skidded to a halt on the top step.

The door to a bedroom was open.

A hand flopped down the side of the bed.

They might still be alive.

He fell, stumbling forward.

Was this how people felt once they discovered his targets?

How many times had he produced this feeling in someone?

Shut up.

Those thoughts weren't helpful.

After all, he didn't know they were dead.

But as soon as he entered the room, he knew.

Elsie lay alone.

Eyes wide.

Body spread over the bloody duvet.

Multiple lines along her throat.

That's the thing the movies don't tell you — it isn't as easy as it looks to slit someone's throat. For those who weren't experts in killing like him, it might take three, four, maybe even five times to sink a knife in deep enough and kill someone.

Well, whoever had done this had made sure.

Cassy.

He rushed through the hallway, glancing into the empty bathroom as he made his way into the child's bedroom.

It was empty. Tidy. Organised.

Untouched.

This could be good.

Or it could be bad.

He pounded back down the stairs, tearing out of the door and through to the barn.

He saw the foot before he saw the rest of the corpse.

A foot with Connor's boot on.

Another body left to rot.

Fresh blood glistening beneath a line across the throat. Pieces of a broken 1960 Les Paul Gibson next to a bruised head.

And, as he fell to his knees, the thought returned: *is this how it feels?*

He'd seen and made hundreds of dead bodies.

But this was different.

This body was harder to see. So much so, he had to turn his head away.

How stupid he was.

How inept.

Cassy.

He went back through the house, searching every wardrobe, every hiding place, then searching them again. She was not there.

He returned to the barn and reached into Connor's pocket. The left pocket was empty, but the right pocket wasn't. He retrieved the keys to Connor's Volkswagen Sharan.

It wasn't a racer, nor was it a jeep, or even anything resembling the car those bastards had. But it would do.

It was a family car, made for families. So what would it matter if that was destroyed too?

He unlocked the car and took hold of the steering wheel. The sun made him squint, so he lifted down the visor. Attached to it was a picture. Connor, a few years younger, with a toddler Cassy and a healthy Elsie.

Sullivan growled. He wasn't aware of doing it, he just did.

He sped off, marking his wake with dirt, driving faster down the country lanes than the car could take.

CHAPTER TWENTY-ONE

SULLIVAN ACCELERATED HARD, DETERMINED TO CATCH UP with Connor and Elsie's killers. He didn't just drive quickly; he drove recklessly. He knew his anger was taking control and he tried to quell it, tried to think rationally. He wanted to be at his best, and that required him to think clearly.

It didn't take long until he saw them in the distance. Black car. Driving under the speed limit to avoid suspicion, just like he used to — not that there was anyone to be suspicious in these deserted country roads. But when one has just performed a hit, one takes no risks.

He sped up, gaining on them, getting closer and closer. They were nearing the end of the single-track lane, almost at the main road, and Sullivan had no intention of letting them reach it.

He mounted the grass verge, lurched the car past them, and blocked their route. They didn't slow down quickly enough, and he knocked their bonnet, forcing them to spiral into a grassy verge.

Though he did not knock them too hard – Cassy might be in the car.

He was out of the car and marching toward them before their car had finished spinning. As soon as the vehicle became still, he opened the passenger door, grabbed the guy by the throat, and threw him out.

The man fell onto his back, but his disorientation didn't delay his responses for long. He withdrew his knife and swung it.

Sullivan grabbed the wrist, twisted the arm, stood on the neck.

He could break the arm.

He could take the knife.

He could damage the spine.

But none of them would give him the satisfaction that this man's death would provide.

Hearing the car doors behind him open, he took the knife from the whimpering man's hand, dropped to his knee, and stuck it upwards through the base of the guy's throat.

Three hooligans emerged from the car, ready for him. Bruised from the collision. Knives out, staring at the body he had just created.

"You is gonna regret that!" claimed the one Sullivan had spoken to earlier. The one with *fuck* and *cunt* on his knuckles. As he came closer, Sullivan saw three tear drops tattooed beside his left eye.

Normally, Sullivan would dispatch the leader first. He'd want to scare the others off by killing the scariest one. This time, however, he would not — he had a feeling that this one would be the one with the information Sullivan needed, so he decided he'd leave this one until last.

Besides, this one would give Sullivan the most satisfaction when he squealed.

"Where's the girl?" Sullivan asked.

None of them said anything.

"Where is she?"

They approached, slowly. Their faces angry, like they believed it was intimidating. They thought they had strength in numbers. They thought this would be easy.

Fucking idiots.

Tattoo Knuckles approached first, swinging, and Sullivan ducked. Sullivan swung a fist upwards, striking it into the underside of Tattoo Knuckle's chin with enough force to send him to his back, leaving him to waver in and out of consciousness while he dealt with the other two.

Idiot 1 approached with his knife aimed for Sullivan's cheek. Sullivan ducked and took out Idiot 1's feet, landing him next to the car. He opened the car door, lifted Idiot 1's head, and pounded the car door against his skull.

He wanted a few more strikes with the car door, but Idiot 2 came at him, swinging his knife. Sullivan caught the guy's wrist and twisted until his palm opened, and the knife fell. He kept hold of the man's arm, brought it over his back and threw him over his shoulder, landing his head next to the car wheel. In a swift movement, he reached in and released the handbrake, allowing the car to begin to drift down the sloping road.

He sat on the edge of the car seat while the wheel flattened Idiot 2's head, holding onto Idiot 1's shirt so he could drag him along the ground and pound the car door against his cranium while the car drifted.

Just as the car picked up speed, he reapplied the handbrake. He stepped out of the car and surveyed the damage.

Idiot 1's skull was dented and contorted.

Idiot 2's skull was also crushed, though his body still seemed to wriggle. He picked up Idiot 2's stray knife and put him out of his misery.

Sullivan returned to Tattoo Knuckles, who rolled over, groaning at what must be a considerable pain in his head. Sullivan didn't approach him yet. Instead, he held out his arm to indicate what he'd done to his comrades.

Tattoo Knuckles snarled defiantly, though Sullivan was sure it was bravado. His arms were shaking, and he was toughing it out, like these guys do. But, eventually, the sight of his dead friends and the pain Sullivan was about to inflict would make him talk.

"Cassy," Sullivan stated. "Where is she?

"Who the fuck is you?"

Sullivan tutted. "Is you? We really need to do something with your diction."

"What?"

Sullivan sighed. "I said you're a dick, son."

The guy looked confused again. "... eh?"

"Not the brightest fella, are you?"

Sullivan strode forward, and Tattoo Knuckles backed away.

Then he stopped backing away, as if a sting of pride told him that, despite witnessing three murders, he should never back away from anyone.

By the time he'd thought to aim his knife, Sullivan had taken it from him and sliced it downwards from Tattoo Knuckles' shoulder to wrist.

He fell, rolled over, grabbing his bicep, trying to push himself up with his one good arm.

Sullivan took this momentary respite to reach into his pocket and pull out his pills. His chest was hurting again, but once he medicated, he was ready to continue.

Sullivan was briefly distracted by a banging noise coming from the boot of the car. He considered opening it, then decided he needed to finish with Tattoo Knuckles first.

"What's your name?" Sullivan asked.

Raul shook his head. Looked at his friends. His face curled into anger. Normally this was the point at which one would beg for their life. This man was taking a little while to get there.

"I said, what's your name?"

"Go fuck yourself."

Sullivan swung the knife into Tattoo Knuckle's side, just below the ribs, and slid it back out.

This prompted a cry of anguish. Sullivan saw a flicker of that fear he wished to inspire.

"What is your–"

"Raul! It's fucking Raul."

"Why did you murder that family?"

Raul peered at the corpses behind Sullivan, then up at Sullivan, a mixture of anger and terror in his eyes. His adrenaline was running out.

Finally, despair took over, and he answered.

"'Cause we was told to."

Sullivan nodded.

"By who?"

Raul looked down.

Sullivan remembered this look. It was the look of someone trying to decide which was scarier: the man he worked for, or the man demanding to know who he worked for.

Give away his boss, he'd face death. Say no to Sullivan, and he'd face pain then death.

Perhaps he needed a little more persuading.

Sullivan swung the knife into the side of Raul's thigh.

He held it there.

Put his face so close to Raul's he could feel the onions in his breath.

"Who?"

"Hugo."

"Hugo what?"

"Hugo Jones. Please, he'll kill me–"

Sullivan pulled the knife out and Raul rolled onto his front, screaming in the kind of agony Sullivan knew would make a man give up anything: his boss, his credit card number, even his wife's bra size.

Anything.

"Where can I find Hugo?"

"Birmingham. He runs everything there... Please, just stop..."

"Does he have a business address?"

"What?"

"I want to find him."

"You don't. Trust me, you don't know who you're fucking with."

Sullivan crouched down, took hold of Raul's hair, and lifted his head up.

"I can't walk away," said Sullivan. "You see, it's kinda my thing."

"Fine," said Raul, and gave up an address. Sullivan wanted more than one location where he could search for this Hugo Jones, but Cassy had been in that boot for long enough. He dug the knife into Raul's throat, forcing it further and further in, until he had lodged it as far in as it would go. With all the strength he had, he pulled it across, dragging it until blood streamed down his fingers.

As he waited for Raul's body to stop twitching, Sullivan opened the passenger door and reached into the drop down. He pulled out a SatNav, switched it on and scrolled through the various recent addresses. There was the address Raul had given up, plus a few more. A flat, a warehouse and an M6 service station appeared a few times, so he made a mental note of those locations.

He returned the SatNav to the drop down and walked to the boot. He lifted it, making sure he stood the opposite side to the four dead bodies; he did not want Cassy to see them.

Cassy leapt up and threw her arms around him.

"Close your eyes," Sullivan whispered in her ear.

She did as he asked and kept them shut tight. He carried her to the back seat of the Bugatti the imbeciles had been driving, then sat in the front. He drove further along the road, just far enough that she wouldn't see the carnage, then stopped, turned and looked to her.

"You can open your eyes now."

She opened them.

He reached his hand out and placed it on hers. She squeezed it with both hands, holding it tightly.

"They hurt Grandad and Grandma, we have to go back! We have to help them!"

Sullivan looked down.

Fuck.

How did he explain this?

"Please, we have to—"

"Cassy," he interrupted. "It — it's too late."

She stared into his eyes, and in that stare, he felt regret.

Regret for every child he had ever made look like that.

For every orphan who had to learn their parents were dead because of him.

For every moment of sadness he had created in so many children.

"But..."

A solitary tear drifted down her cheek, preceding more cries.

Either she'd be strong, and she'd power through these feelings, or even use the pain to inspire her. She would use the memory to do good in this world.

Or she'd be human. She would be in shock and wouldn't quite realise what had happened. Grief isn't like it is in the movies; it isn't blatant. It's subtle. It spreads through you slowly, only manifesting at the most inopportune moments.

She would grow up hurting.

And she would never recover.

"Look, I—" Sullivan went to say, but said nothing.

Her eyes hadn't left his. They'd barely blinked.

Her body was shaking.

Her face was pale.

"We'll get who did this, I promise," Sullivan assured her, as if that meant anything.

As if vengeance would ever stop the pain, or do anything to bring them back.

BIRMINGHAM CITY CENTRE, ENGLAND

CHAPTER TWENTY-TWO

EACH STEP HUGO TOOK WAS DELIBERATE, EACH BREATH intentional, and each glare thought-out.

Whoever brought him bad news would do so against their better instincts. They would dread telling him where the car was found, and the bodies that were found around it. They would hate having to bring him news that would prompt such lethal wrath.

But someone had to bring him bad news — as to not deliver such information would be even worse.

"It was in Frome, about three or four miles from the farm."

Hugo stood by the window. Below him was the giant eyesore of Birmingham – the Selfridges building. A bunch of silver dots in an odd shape. It was like they tried to 'do Birmingham up,' but, in doing so, they just made it appear far tackier than it previously did. It was like trying to paint a smile on a corpse; it may smile, but after a while the stink would still be too much.

"The good news," Darren went to say, brushing his untidy, floppy hair out of his eyes. He could sense the grimace on Hugo's face, despite staring at his back.

"I mean, if there is any good news in such a situation..." Darren corrected himself and trailed off.

Still no response.

Hugo's cat meandered from the kitchen and into the room. It walked casually to Hugo's leg and rubbed itself against his shin. Looked up at him like Hugo owed it something.

"The couple who gave a home to Nathaniel are dead. This attack happened after they were executed."

Hugo looked down at the cat.

It stared back. Meowed. Maybe it was hungry.

"The girl is missing, however. I assume whoever did this took her."

Hugo took a deep breath through his nose, held it, and let it out.

No matter what went on in his mind, it was crucial that he was the epitome of calm. He sensed Darren's nervous stare, his wariness, as if Hugo was going to turn around and unleash his fury.

But Hugo did not.

He kept his hands behind his back. Stood still. Looked at the cat pawing at his leg.

"The police are making enquiries, they got to the scene first."

More bad news.

The cat meowed again.

"We have the money it would take to pin it on someone they have already convicted, or to leave it unsolved, or — or whatever you want. We're just waiting for your instructions. As soon as you give the go ahead..."

Hugo wasn't listening anymore. He was looking at his cat.

Although, technically, it was Nathaniel's cat.

Somehow, after inheriting his son's worthless possessions, he had also inherited his cat.

His wife liked this cat.

Hugo did not.

"Sir?" Darren prompted.

The cat meowed again.

What the fuck did it want?

"Sir, what would you like us to do?"

The cat still stared back. Not blinking. Like a childish competition. Like some kind of game.

"Sir, if we could–"

Hugo grabbed the cat by its neck in a quick, chaotic scramble. He held his arm back, as if he was about to throw a cricket ball. He swung the cat's head into the window.

It cried.

He swung it again.

And again.

Until the cat made no more noise.

An imprint of blood dirtied an otherwise immaculate pane of glass.

He opened the window and threw the dead cat out, leaving it for someone below to deal with.

Hugo turned to Darren.

Hugo was still. There was wrath there, but the fact that it was so well concealed, kept so succinctly under the skin, only made the image of his lucid annoyance all the more unsettling.

"Clean that off," he said. "And get me whoever did this. I want them before the day is out. No one kills four of my people and gets away with it that easily. There will be a trace. Use it."

He charged away, freeing Darren from his anger, slamming the door behind him.

111

ASTON, BIRMINGHAM, ENGLAND

CHAPTER TWENTY-THREE

As Sullivan left the M5 and entered the M6, signs for Birmingham grew more frequent, and large buildings typical of a city surrounded them.

Sullivan was tired. His chest was hurting. And Cassy hadn't said a single word. She had sat there, the entire journey, in the back, seatbelt on, staring ahead. Empty expression, wide eyes. He wasn't even sure he'd seen her blink.

After he passed signs declaring they were now in Birmingham, he exited the motorway and drove to the nearest town, passing Villa Park as he did.

Although, as they approached, he decided *town* was an ambitious term to describe the place. A few stores ran up a street, most of them charity shops or bookies. A few grown men in matching grey tracksuits gathered around a lamppost, smoking. An old lady who probably looked a lot older than she was hobbled up the street on her walker. A few men speaking Polish walked past a graffitied bus shelter.

Deciding he'd been to worse places, Sullivan pulled into the car park of a pub called *The Queen's Nose*.

And he waited.

He knew never to just get out of a car. A habit from his old life. After an assassination, you were most vulnerable. The subsequent hours were the most likely time for you to be killed in retaliation.

Sullivan was sure no one had tailed him. Was sure no one had seen him. Was sure he was safe.

But he was driving their car.

An intentional move. A way of saying *fuck you* to whoever had ordered the hit.

A way of showing the ones who had killed...

He shook his head.

He couldn't even conclude the thought.

All those years of killing unknown targets, and he couldn't even finish a sentence in his mind about what he'd witnessed.

Had he come to care for that family?

Or was the trauma of his former career dirtying his mind?

He stopped his inner monologue. The rambles could wait for later. For now, he had to do his check.

Two other cars were in the car park. One of them was dirty and grey, although he was sure grey wasn't the car's original colour. The car hadn't been touched in months, at least.

The other car was a Ford. It missed a wing mirror.

A few men walked past. More tracksuits.

A woman with missing teeth held onto the hand of a child trying to run.

Then nothing.

It was safe.

"Come on," Sullivan said. He stepped out of the car, shut the door, and reached for Cassy's hand.

Her hand wasn't there. She was still in the car.

With a sigh, he opened the door to the backseat and crouched.

She still didn't move.

"Cassy," Sullivan said.

Nothing.

"Cassy, I need you to move."

Still nothing.

"Cassy!"

Not even a blink.

"For fuck's sake, Cassy, we don't have time for–"

He stopped himself. Dropped his head. He shouldn't talk to her like this.

He just wasn't used to dealing with kids.

Hell, he wasn't used to talking to people. Never mind someone vulnerable and in shock.

"Cassy," he tried, reaching out for her hand.

She flinched.

Her arm was stiff. Cold. If he hadn't seen her move, he would think she was dead.

"This isn't good enough, Cassy, we don't know who's about, we have to get in–"

He stopped himself.

He was doing it again.

Being impatient.

He just did not understand how to deal with this.

He was just about to say *well fucking stay in the car then* but stopped and reminded himself once more: Kid. Vulnerable. Shocked.

Family murdered before her.

She wasn't used to the sight of death like he was.

But what was he supposed to do?

"Cassy, I need to protect you, they might be looking for you. The only way to do that is if you come with me."

Nothing.

"Cassy, we — just — we need — fucking *come on!*"

He stood, punched the side of the car, and turned around.

Ran his hand through his hair.

This was why he was a nomad. He couldn't deal with people. Or kids. Or trauma.

He didn't know how to speak to a person anymore.

He crouched. Ran his hands through his hair. Turned back to the car.

She'd moved. Now, she was looking at him. Her lip quivering. Eyelids flickering.

She looked like everything she contained was about to explode.

And then she spoke.

"You really think they are coming after us?"

Sullivan didn't know what to say, so he nodded. An empty nod.

"And are they really... gone?"

He rushed into the car, took the seat next to her, and put his arms around her. He placed her head on his chest. A hand in her hair. A hand on her back. Holding tightly. Firmly.

And she cried.

Oh boy, how she cried.

Everything came out. Every image, every moment of fear, every thought and emotion she had rejected — it came out in waves and floods.

"It's okay," he said. "It's okay."

And he didn't rush her.

Didn't move her.

He stayed like this for the next hour, maybe longer, he didn't know, and he didn't care.

He held her like this for as long as she needed.

And they didn't leave the car and enter the pub until she was ready.

CHAPTER TWENTY-FOUR

THE PUB HAD ADVERTISED FOOD OUTSIDE, BUT IT WAS NOT somewhere you'd go for a family meal.

A few men sat glumly at the bar, two tattooed men in vests played pool, and a man with few teeth cleaned a pint glass.

He took Cassy by the hand, keeping her close, into a booth in the far corner. He passed another man sat alone at a table; this man looked a little classier than the others, but that still wasn't saying much. He wore glasses and a light-coloured shirt. He was alone.

Once Cassy was settled, he walked over to the bar. The barman stared at him.

"It said outside you do food," Sullivan said.

The barman took a piece of paper from beside the till and put it in front of Sullivan. There were four choices written on a single A4 piece of paper. Curry, hamburger, lasagne or hot dog. Sullivan imagined these were all items that could be done in a microwave.

"I'll take the hamburger," he said. "And two waters."

The barman poured the waters and placed them on the bar.

"We'll be sat over there. In the booth."

Sullivan walked back to where Cassy sat.

Silence consumed the place. It felt like a wake that no one cared about. He wished to talk to Cassy, but he feared being overheard.

Eventually, he turned to her and whispered.

"Do you have any other relatives?"

Cassy shrugged.

"No one? No other set of grandparents? Aunts? Uncles? Cousins? Anything?"

She shrugged again.

"Do you have any friends who have parents you are close to?"

"I have a friend from school. Francesca. But her parents aren't very nice."

School.

The sudden thought she could not go back to her school felt awful. She had no idea what her life would be like now. She did not understand how much she would have to let go of.

Then again, what other option did he have?

Whoever did the hit wouldn't let Cassy live. Not after what she'd witnessed. She needed protection.

What happened to her parents was a vicious hit. They were killed deliberately and by people who meant it. He knew, because he used to perform hits just like them.

But what if he couldn't find the man who ordered the death of her family? The next best outcome for her would be a new life, with the kind of solitude Sullivan was so accustomed to; which was probably only marginally better than death.

She sat so quietly and sweetly, with no idea of the world he occupied and she had just entered.

She couldn't stay with him.

Not after what had happened to Talia.

Bad things happened to those he cared about.

The barman brought over a hamburger. Sullivan thanked him and was treated to a grunt in response.

Sullivan placed his hand on the chips beside the burger. Lukewarm. The bun around the burger was still hard. The burger looked to have no meat in it.

This wasn't the sort of place he was used to dining in, but they just needed somewhere to stop. Hide. Think. And feed Cassy.

Cassy devoured the meal. She ate it so quickly Sullivan couldn't imagine she'd been able to take in its bad taste.

As she ate, Sullivan asked the barman if he could use their phone. After a long, unimpressed glare, the barman handed it over, and Sullivan returned to his seat.

One useful advantage of his old work was the contacts he'd made. There weren't many who would still talk to him now, but there was one man he could call.

And, seeing as he had a bit of time to kill, he may as well call him.

After a few rings, a tired voice answered.

"Hello?"

"Marty, this is Jay Sullivan."

Marty was a very useful man.

"Jay Sullivan! Oh my god, back from the dead, tell me it isn't so, Mr Jayo Sullivano!"

And, oh yeah, Marty was annoying as hell.

"Sorry I've not been in touch."

"Hey, we all got our eggs to fry, it's good to hear from you."

"I need a favour."

"Well, I owe you about twenty favourinos, so spill it, brother, what do you need?"

Sullivan sighed. He hated phoning this man, and he was wondering whether it was worth it, but no one knew cars and traffic like Marty. You tell him a car, he will tell you the history — and not just the history google would tell you. He would tell you where it had been picked up by traffic cameras, the detailed history of previous owners, and frequent locations the car had travelled to.

"I need history on a car."

"I'm your man! Hit me with that licence plate."

Sullivan peered out the window at the Buggati waiting in the car park. He read the licence plate out.

"Brillo mateyo, just give the computer a minute or five."

"Okay."

"Meanwhile, tell me, how have you been? What's the deal? What's the dish? What is up with Mr Jay Sullivan?"

"Probably best I don't share my stories."

"Incognito? I dig it. Hold up, I'm getting results."

Sullivan looked to Cassy and her empty plate,

"Right. It is owned by a Raul Spencer. What a weird name. That's like a proper mix of cultures right there."

"Who is he?"

"Got a police record. Did three years for dealing. A drink driving offence that was brushed under the carpet. Convictions of GBH and assault, but no prison time for that. That's unusual, ain't it?"

"Yes."

"Sounded like someone was giving good money to stop him returning to prison. The man Raul worked for must be well rich. Raul did time in Brighton, but never in Birmingham, where all his offences came to nothing. Oh, wait one moment. Something new just flashed up."

"What?"

"He's deceased."

So they'd found the body.

That meant whoever Connor and Elsie's killers worked for would now know someone had killed his men and taken Cassy.

"Tell me about the car."

"Okay. Let's see here... Was reported stolen. But it wasn't."

"What do you mean?"

"As in, the car was stolen, but that was wiped. As in, I'm looking at deleted data you wouldn't see from looking at the copper's database. Jeeze, Sullivan, this man is jacked up. Whatever he's doing, he's got connections in all the right places. They have to be well paid to delete that kind of shit."

"Any links to any other criminals?"

"A few, but only one that's consistent."

"Who's that?"

"Hugo Jones."

"And what can you tell me about him?"

"Nothing, man."

"Just tell me whatever's there, I'll decide if it's nothing."

"No, as in nothing. I'm going back, like, through his whole life, and nothing. He's never been charged. There are loads of people linked to him with arrests for all kinds of shit, but nothing on him. His record is clean. That either means he's a saint, or..."

"Or he's never been arrested or charged."

"Can't be. I've never seen this before. For someone to escape huge offences or have nothing I can find..."

Sullivan sighed.

"There's got to be someone who can tell me something about him," he said.

"Maybe you should just leave this one. If he's had the police on side for this long, he'd probably even be outside the Falcon's price range."

"Thanks, Marty," he said, ignoring his friend's concern.

"I'm being serious. No one will go after him. You take on this guy, then... you do it on your own."

Sullivan couldn't help but grin.

As if he had any other way.

CHAPTER TWENTY-FIVE

SULLIVAN GAZED AROUND THE DECREPIT PUB. IT WAS A PLACE where nomads drank. Lowlifes with no reason to be anywhere but drinking alone in a darkened pub. As dubious as these people may seem, they were likely to be the kind of people who had experienced the darker sides to the city. Perhaps they had heard of Hugo Jones.

Once Cassy had finished eating, and they were ready to go, Sullivan walked up to the bar. Remaining aware of what was around him, he readied himself to ask the question.

"Hey," he said to the barman, who turned his head. Everyone scowled, as if talking in this pub was the most abominable act known to mankind. "Have you ever heard of Hugo Jones?"

The silence became even more silent. Glasses were placed on tables, sips ceased, and every set of eyes focussed on him.

The barman leant in, and spoke quietly — even though every person in the pub could hear.

"Who are you?" the barman asked, his voice gruff and coarse.

"Just a man."

"Well, Just A Man, don't go asking questions like that here. We don't want to get involved in nothing. You understand?"

Sullivan looked over his shoulder. Scanned the pub. The two blokes playing pool had stopped. The old man in the corner hovered his glass halfway to his mouth. These stares weren't just stares, or even glares. They were sinister gapes of disbelief. They were looking at him with grave shock and severe apprehension.

"I just want to know–"

"We know nothing," said the man on the barstool closest to him, with a conviction hard to argue with.

These people would not talk.

Besides, their reaction had told him everything he needed to know.

He placed some cash on the bar and nodded at Cassy. She followed.

As did someone else.

Out the corner of his eye, Sullivan saw the man sat on his own wearing glasses and a checked shirt finish his pint, get up, and follow their steps.

Sullivan paused and, as the man walked out, he took the man's collar and pushed him against the wall by his throat.

The man held his hands up.

"Please," the man said, his voice shaking. "Please, don't hurt me."

This didn't seem like a man who'd ever been in a fight. In fact, he looked like the kind of man who would apologise to someone who spilled a pint on him to avoid a fight. His mannerisms were jolty and strange, his face was a constant flicker between despair and humiliation, and he dressed like an oversized child.

Sullivan used his spare hand to pat the man down, checking every pocket, every bit of material, every crevasse. He was clean.

He let the man go and stepped back.

"Why did you want to know about Hugo Jones?" the man asked.

"Just interested, why?"

The man looked at Cassy, then at Sullivan.

"Follow me," the man said, and walked up the street.

"Where?"

The man paused. "We can't talk about this in the open."

"Where do you propose?"

"My flat. It will be safe there. Really."

Sullivan looked to Cassy, mouthed *it's okay,* and they both followed.

CHAPTER TWENTY-SIX

SULLIVAN PAID ATTENTION TO EVERY PART OF THE JOURNEY. Every step up the stone stairs, along the balcony, and into the flat.

He kept Cassy behind him, his hand on her arm, peering back and forth at all times. He remained wary. It was hard for him not to be — he observed things the average person doesn't. It was hardly something he could turn off.

Most people would notice a mass of flats and chain-smoking residents and sounds of kids arguing. Not everyone would notice that the flat three doors down had a new lock on an old door. Not everyone would see that the teenager hanging around a few doors down wore jacket and trousers from Primark, but with Gucci Logo Rhyton Trainers worth £700. And not everyone in their situation would question the eager-ness with which the man was bringing them back to this flat.

The man's flat smelt like sweat and beer. The curtains were drawn. Cracks marked the wall. A smoke detector sat on the table.

They moved into what Sullivan assumed to be the living room area — an assumption made by the sight of a television and a sofa; not the empty plates, discarded clothes and stained pint glasses.

Upon a windowsill, and a cupboard, and on the wall above an armchair, were photos of this man and a woman. Blond, pretty, beautiful smile. Yet, as Sullivan looked through to the bathroom, he only saw one toothbrush. A toilet seat left up. A single towel dumped on the floor.

The man locked the front door and turned to Sullivan. He was jittery. Some may assume he was on drugs. Sullivan did not. He was nervous. On edge. Suddenly anxious about these two strangers in this flat, and what he was about to tell them. Over his shoulder, there was a lanyard hung on a coat-hanger displaying the NHS logo.

"My name is Doctor Charles Allen," he said.

Sullivan squinted at the lanyard, and the badge confirmed this name.

"What do I call you?" Charles asked.

"Whatever you want."

Sullivan walked to the window, keeping hold of Cassy. He moved the curtain slightly and looked out. A bunch of kids hung around a garage. A guy wearing a cap pissed in a bush.

"You live here?" Sullivan asked.

"Yes."

"Doesn't look much like a doctor's place."

"What would a doctor's place look like?"

"I don't know. A little healthier."

Charles snorted a laugh.

Sullivan wasn't joking.

"Can I get you a drink?" Charles asked, meandering to the kitchen. The flat was open plan, which meant Sullivan could keep watching him.

Sullivan was about to say no, then remembered Cassy may want something. He looked to Cassy, who stared back at him with a wary expression that Sullivan interpreted as *I want to get out of here*.

"No."

Charles re-approached with a glass of water for himself.

"Suit yourself. Please, sit."

Charles sat in the armchair, leaving Sullivan and Cassy to perch on the end of a sofa, trying to stay away from the stains.

"You said you could help us," Sullivan said.

"Uh huh."

"With Hugo Jones."

"What do you want with Hugo?"

Sullivan studied Charles. His knee was bouncing. He was sweating. His face crumbled, then flickered back to normality. Every now and then he would glance at one of the pictures he had spread around the flat.

This wasn't someone being distrustful. This was someone in the middle of severe grief. Sullivan had been exactly the same, many years ago, after his wife was murdered in front of him.

"What did he do to her?" Sullivan asked.

"What?"

"Hugo. What did he do to your wife?"

"How did you…"

"The pictures. You keep looking at them. I assume it is your wife?"

Charles looked down. He cleaned his glasses.

"What was her name?" Sullivan asked.

"Nancy."

"And what did he do to her?"

Charles looked to the corner of the room. Looked anywhere but at Sullivan.

"This girl has just watched her grandparents die," Sullivan said, and felt Cassy flinch beside her. "Because of Hugo Jones. And I may be the only one who can protect her. Tell me what he did."

Charles took a deep breath. Held it.

"He... killed her," he said on his outward breath. "I owed money."

"How much?"

"Thirty thousand."

"That all? He killed her for that?"

"He made the threat. His men made the threat. He kept saying it, but I never quite... I was in debt with the bank. Three of them. No one would give me another loan to repay him. In the end..."

"How did he do it?"

Charles looked astonished.

"I have to know," Sullivan said. "I need an idea what I'm up against."

"You can't beat him."

"I don't plan to beat him. I plan to kill him."

"No one kills Hugo."

"We'll see."

"You don't understand."

"With all due respect, Doctor – *you* don't understand. How did he kill her?"

Charles cleaned his glasses again.

"I'm sure those glasses are clean by now. How did she die?"

"He – he texted me from her phone. Told me she was planning something romantic. To come home with a bottle of wine. And when I came home... Roses led me through the flat... It was in quite a better state than this, this was only meant to be temporary, we would get a house if it weren't for the debt... Candles lit the doorway to the bedroom, and they surrounded the room. I thought it was the most romantic thing in the world, and then... There she was. On the bed. I thought she was joking at first, but the blood had crusted and she..."

"That's okay."

Sullivan stood.

He turned to Cassy.

He either had to leave her here, or in the car outside wherever he was to confront Hugo.

He really did not want to leave her with this man, but she was safer here than with him. There was no reason for Hugo to return here. They'd already killed his wife. Charles may be unhinged, but he was weak. It would be okay.

"I need her to stay with you," Sullivan said.

"What?"

"I will find this Hugo, then I'll come back and–"

"You won't. You won't come back. If you so much as say a nasty word to him, you won't–"

"No!" Cassy cried, grabbing onto Sullivan's arm.

Sullivan crouched in front of her.

"I don't know him, he's strange."

"I know, but where I am going is not safe. I will be a few hours, then I'll be back."

"But–"

"If I don't do this, you'll never be safe."

She went to argue but didn't.

Sullivan turned to Charles.

"If she is hurt in any way, you will be next. You understand?"

He nodded.

Cassy looked back at him with those child's eyes. So vulnerable. So unaware.

Those eyes did not understand the horrors they were capable of seeing.

"I promise," he said. "I won't let you get hurt."

He turned. Walked away. Forced himself not to look back.

If he had to look at those eyes again, there would be no way he'd ever leave.

BIRMINGHAM CITY CENTRE, UNITED KINGDOM

CHAPTER TWENTY-SEVEN

SULLIVAN HAD A FEW LOCATIONS TO LOOK BASED ON WHAT HE found out from Raul and the SatNav. Two addresses, a warehouse, and an M6 service station were his starting points.

The M6 service station would be the last place he'd try — it would be a large location with many places Hugo could be. He'd be far better off looking in more isolated places on the list.

Only problem was, Sullivan had no idea what this Hugo guy looked like.

If he was as powerful as everyone claimed, however, it wouldn't be that difficult to identify him. He would expect some smug bastard in a bastard suit, walking around like a bastard with people treating him like he was the messiah.

He used to get excited about this kind of hit.

He never knew his targets, or what they had done to warrant death. It was not in his job remit. The Falcons would send him a picture, a name, and sometimes a method of death. But when he received someone like this, someone who he knew was frequently killing and harming the innocent, he knew the person deserved it.

The first place was a warehouse. It looked to be in use, but that's how Hugo Jones would want it to appear. Trucks would rotate the parking spaces outside. People would move boxes in and out, but they would be the same boxes, and the same people. All things to throw people off any suspicion that this place was being used for anything other than your average warehouse was used for.

He waited outside for an hour, almost two. There was no evidence that anything was happening here, so he moved on.

The next address was a flat in a building opposite the ugly Selfridges building.

The flat itself was seven stories up. The window was open. But there was no movement past either of the two visible windows.

He waited for an hour. He had no binoculars — he was just looking for movement of light. Something to indicate life.

Nothing.

There was one more place.

A house. A family home just north of Birmingham City Centre, in a place called Sutton Coldfield. Up the A38 and onto a smaller A road.

He spun the car back onto the road, past Villa Park, and onward past Star City.

He drove at the speed limit, not attracting attention.

He was still driving the Bugatti. If he wanted the surprise element, he would need to ditch it and proceed on foot.

Then again, wouldn't it be a brilliant *fuck you* for this Hugo guy to look out of his family home and see the car of his four dead lackeys waiting outside?

Sullivan had to be professional. Go in for the kill, protect Cassy. But he couldn't help being excited at the idea of toying with this man.

Grinning, he continued off the A38 and onto Sutton New Road, past a town called Erdington.

He was almost there.

SUTTON COLDFIELD, NORTH OF BIRMINGHAM, ENGLAND

CHAPTER TWENTY-EIGHT

Sunday lunch was a beautiful British tradition, and one that Hugo insisted on. No matter what was going on with business, whatever feud he had entered or whatever operation was occurring, he insisted on it.

His wife would cook a perfect piece of meat; beef, or a loin of pork, or a chicken, or sometimes even lamb. She would accompany it with steamed vegetables, thick cauliflower cheese, and an assortment of stuffing balls.

Hugo would sit at the head of the table, of course. His wife, Charlene, to his right. His eldest son to his left and his other three children at the end of the table. They would bounce conversation back and forth, engage in meaningless chat, and joke like a happy family does. He would find out what his children were doing at school, what Charlene had done in her latest book club meeting or whatever she did, and it would give him a chance to be a father.

Sundays, however, had not felt the same for a few months now.

Hugo wanted it to feel the same. He wished for the old times; for the happy nattering of conversation. But Charlene barely spoke anymore. She cooked the meal then kept her head down, not looking at her husband, but occasionally glancing at the empty seat to Hugo's left.

The seat where their eldest son previously sat.

Because of this, his children didn't talk much. And he did not appreciate Charlene influencing the children in such a way.

"This is a good meal," Hugo said, attempting once again to talk to Charlene.

Charlene nodded; a small nod one could have easily missed.

"How is book club?"

"Fine," she muttered, in a voice so low it was like it was hidden away somewhere.

"And the children, how was their parent's evening?"

Still, she didn't look at her husband. "Good."

"What are your plans this week?"

She shrugged.

Hugo slammed his fist upon the table, causing the dishes of vegetables to jump up, and for his children to cease eating.

"Children," Hugo addressed them, in a slow, particular voice; a voice that sounded restrained and polite, but was anything but. "Please would you take your meal and go upstairs to eat?"

The children looked to their father, confused.

"Now."

They did not need to be asked again. They took their plates, rushed out of the room, and the sound of them running up the stairs grew faint.

Hugo allowed the silence to grow. He appreciated the power of a silence. The weak filled awkward silences with endless speech. The powerful allowed the silence to fester and grow.

Charlene did not look at him. Nor did she eat. Or even move. She sat, hunched over her plate, occasionally glancing at the empty seat.

"I want you to say it," Hugo said.

Charlene mumbled something.

"Excuse me?"

"Say what?" she finally said, only just audibly.

"You keep glancing at that seat like you have every Sunday for the past few weeks. Why don't you say what you want to say?"

"There's nothing I want to–"

Hugo slammed his fist upon the table again.

Charlene jumped.

She covered her face to hide the tears.

"Don't you fucking cry," Hugo said. "You know what he did."

She shook her head. There was much Hugo could see she wanted to say, but she was too scared.

Good.

She should be scared.

Everyone should be.

He did not tolerate this insolence. Not from his inferiors, not from his victims, and definitely not from his damn wife.

"Why don't you say what it is you want to say?"

She didn't.

"You think I shouldn't have killed him. That he didn't deserve it."

She bit her lip. Held in the tears.

"You wish he was still alive. Don't you?"

She finally looked at him.

"*Don't you?*"

"Yes!" she gave in. "Yes, I do! He was my son, he was–"

Hugo grabbed the back of her hair and slammed her head into the plate of untouched food. Pieces of carrot fell from her cheek. The plate slid away, and he pressed her face against the table.

Hugo moved his lips to beside her ear.

"He was a traitor," he told her. "He was a traitor, and he deserved to–"

He paused.

Something distracted him.

Outside the window.

He let her go, transfixed.

No...

His walked forward, staring.

It can't be...

Parked outside. Placed there deliberately. Intentionally.

Raul's car.

He took out his phone. Sent a text. Just one word; the word that triggered an emergency response.

It wouldn't take them long.

"Get upstairs with the kids," Hugo told Charlene.

But it was too late.

He turned around.

Charlene's hair was in one hand, and the knife Hugo had used to slice his chicken pressed against his wife's neck.

"You fucking idiot," said Hugo. "You have no idea what you have just done."

CHAPTER TWENTY-NINE

IT HADN'T BEEN DIFFICULT TO SNEAK IN AMONGST THE shouting and the commotion. The backdoor was unlocked, and Sullivan still had enough stealth left to step in without making a sound.

"Get on your knees," Sullivan instructed, pressing the end of the knife against the woman's throat. It wasn't a particularly sharp knife, and it would take a bit of hacking to slit her throat with it. But, with applied strength and speed, he'd manage before Hugo stopped him. And, if Hugo was as skilled as everyone made him out to be, he'd know that.

Hugo was pretty much what Sullivan expected. A smug prick with a cocky smile framed by a grey goatee. He was probably in his fifties and had been running things for a long time; he held himself like a man of experience.

"I said, get on your knees," Sullivan repeated.

Still, Hugo said nothing. Just stood there, looking back. That same grin. That same cocky, self-satisfied grin.

"I said, get on–"

"No."

One word, one syllable. Simple and inelegant. Defiance Sullivan was not used to.

But Sullivan had his wife.

"I will slit her throat," Sullivan said.

"Go ahead. You'd be doing me a favour."

Was he bluffing?

If Sullivan pressed harder, drew blood. Would that prompt Hugo to reconsider?

Hugo strode over to a bookcase.

"Don't move," Sullivan instructed, pressing harder on her neck, allowing a dot of blood to release itself.

Hugo didn't even flinch. He opened a box on the bookcase and removed a gun. A semi-automatic pistol, by the look of it.

Hugo pointed it at Sullivan.

Sullivan moved his body, so he was directly behind Hugo's wife.

Hugo laughed. "I will shoot her to get to you, don't you worry."

"Drop it."

"You're the one who killed my men, are you?"

"I said drop it."

"Where is the girl?"

Shit.

This wasn't going as planned.

He needed to do something quick, but before he had contemplated his options, the backdoor opened behind him.

He glanced over his shoulder and saw men walking in. Three or four, with more coming.

He looked back at Hugo, who aimed the gun at him.

"*You* get on *your* knees," Hugo instructed.

Sullivan considered fighting those behind him.

It would be stupid.

Hugo would shoot him before he had the chance.

Besides, they wanted to know where Cassy was. They would need him alive for that. He had to use that to his advantage.

He let the woman go.

She ran out of the room and pounded up the stairs.

Hugo raised his eyebrows.

Sullivan dropped to his knees. Let go of the knife. Put his hands in the air.

He'd never submitted to anyone before. It didn't feel good. His throat was dry, his chest was hurting, and his humiliation was only just starting.

Hugo walked, slowly and deliberately, toward Sullivan, and pressed the end of his gun against Sullivan's forehead.

"Where is the girl?" he asked.

Sullivan said nothing.

Hugo sighed.

"This is the last time I ask before things get unpleasant. Where is she?"

"Up your arse, you piece of—"

The strike of something hard against the back of his head knocked him onto his front.

He closed his eyes and waited for the initial throbbing to subside.

Another strike came before it did.

And another.

Things went dark.

"Get Phillipe," he heard Hugo say. "We are going to need him."

Who the fuck is Phillipe?

Another knock and Sullivan's mind went blank.

He would find out who Phillipe was very soon.

147

CHAPTER THIRTY

THE FIRST THING SULLIVAN HEARD WAS DRIPPING.

Distant, incessant, rhythmic dripping.

The ominous monotony of imminent damp.

The room was cold. His clothes were gone. His hands were bound.

He could see nothing. He wore a blindfold.

Fuck.

How had he been so stupid?

Had alcohol slowed his mind as much as his body?

Burning.

He smelt burning.

Like hot iron.

Shit…

He'd been in this situation before, with utensils being heated and readied.

He knew what was coming.

"Usually no one takes my clothes off unless I pay them."

"Where is the girl, Jay Sullivan?" asked a French accent.

Ah, so they know my name.

People who knew his name were either deeply involved in

international crime or highly ranked in the government, and he was positive they weren't pals with the prime minister.

"Phillipe, I presume?"

All major crime and government organisations had a Phillipe – though they weren't all called Phillipe. But they were often French. As if a love of baguettes and garlic encouraged a person to derive pleasure in another human's immaculate pain.

He had met many people like Phillipe. They were experts in torture.

One may think you can't be an expert in such a thing, and they would be wrong. It is immensely difficult to cause someone excruciating pain without killing them. You need a deep knowledge of human anatomy, and which parts of the body do what.

Someone like Phillipe could push a pin straight through your throat and avoid death. He could push a blade through your belly in the right place to miss your lungs but scrape along the surface of your stomach, or point at an angle so it just entered the kidney.

Phillipes of the world knew how to cause pain, they knew how to prolong the suffering, and they knew how to extract information.

This Hugo guy must really want Cassy.

Sullivan would have to prepare himself for hell to avoid him getting her.

The best way, he found, to deal with these people — not that he'd ever been on this end of one of their scenes of torture, but he had considered how he'd react should his fortunes ever be so poor — was to meet them with humour.

To keep his wit until the last.

Sullivan had watched people trying to be funny and mock their torturer. The jokes normally stopped after an hour or two.

"What you got cooking?" Sullivan asked. "Smells like bacon."

The answer presented itself against his back. A burning hot iron, like Phillipe was branding a cow. Sullivan allowed himself to scream, as if that would ease the pain somehow. But he knew Phillipe was only gently pressing.

Sullivan knew Phillipe could still press much harder.

"Where is the girl, Jay Sullivan?" Phillipe continued, removing the hot iron.

"Hey, is Hugo in here?"

Silence.

"He is, isn't he?"

Someone huffed.

"Ah, that's him now. Tell him he's a dick. And that I think his wife is hot. Well, moderately hot. I mean, I'd fuck her, but my beer goggles are permanent, you know what I mean?"

The hot iron hit the same place on his back, intensifying the burn. Phillipe pressed a little harder this time, and it stung like a bitch, but the touch was still light.

This had been two minutes.

Sullivan had seen this go on for months.

Even the most stubborn prisoners usually cave after a week or two. The physical pain isn't what does it — it's the psychological torture. The mind can endure far less than the body.

He took a big, deep breath.

Sighed. Grinned. Although he couldn't see Phillipe, he aimed his grin at wherever he thought the fucker was.

He felt the back of his chair.

It was wooden.

Now that was a mistake.

This would be fine to intimidate your average civilian — but people like Sullivan knew how what to look for.

And a wooden chair smashes far better than metal.

There was no use smashing it yet — he wasn't able to tell how many people were in there with him and what weapons they were carrying. The smashing of his chair might be the only opportunity he had, and if he was instantly surrounded by ten guns as soon as he did it, they would make sure they didn't make the same mistake a second time.

He had to be patient.

He had to endure.

For Cassy.

"Where is the girl, Jay Sullivan?"

"Where in France you from, Phillipe? 'Cause I got to say, France is shit enough, but the French... I fucking hate the French. Paris is full of beggars. The Eiffel tower is just a big tower, and honestly, if I want that I'll just pop up to Blackpool."

The hot iron pressed against him harder.

He screamed, but once the initial sting subsided, he morphed it into laughter.

"You are a piece of shit, Phillipe! You really are... I mean, I'm sure you enjoy this, but I'm wondering if this is the best you have."

He heard the movement of items on a metal tray.

More utensils.

There was plenty more to come.

Sullivan sighed.

"Seriously, if we're going to be in here, we should really get to know each other. How much are you packing down there?"

"Excuse me?"

"I just mean, because no one does this kind of shit unless they are compensating. What is it, like, two, three inches?"

"Where is the girl, Jay Sullivan?"

"Up your arse, you French prick."

The sting again. A scream, then laughter.

"Is that the best you got? Is that really it?"

A sigh.

Hugo's voice.

"Can we hurry this up?"

"Perfection cannot be rushed, Mr Jones," replied the French accent. "Give me time, and he will squeal."

"You married, Phillipe?"

"Do you think this is something I haven't heard before, Jay Sullivan? You think this phases me?"

"Oh, come on. Just whip it out. Compare it to mine. Let's see what we're dealing with."

Sullivan heard a different voice. A voice he hadn't heard yet.

"We got her."

"What?"

That last one was Hugo.

"We got her. She's in a house in Aston."

"Are you sure?"

"We just got the call. Sounds legit."

What?

Sullivan panicked.

All the time wasting he was doing, the enduring he was preparing for...

And they had her?

How the hell did they have her?

How had they found out where she was?

"Keep going," said Hugo. "We may still need him if this is fake."

A door opened. Feet shuffled out, then the door closed.

"Ah, Phillipe," said Sullivan. "Alone at last."

ASTON, BIRMINGHAM, ENGLAND

CHAPTER THIRTY-ONE

Cassy didn't trust this man.

But Sullivan had left her with him, and she trusted Sullivan.

He'd made her that guitar.

He'd given her lessons.

He'd saved her from the boot of that car.

Why wouldn't she trust him?

But the more she watched Charles, the more he seemed to fidget. He'd begun by sitting down, his leg bouncing. Then he'd stood and started pacing. Then he'd started opening cupboard doors but taking nothing out of them. Looking out the window, but not looking at anything. Picking up his phone, but never calling.

By the time Cassy's inward panic had heightened, he was walking circles around the living room, charging one way then the other, moving back and forth. He walked around the sofa, around the armchair, stepping over plates and discarded clothes and other things like the television remote and crumbs.

Then there was a knock on the door.

And he suddenly stopped moving.

In fact, he became very, very still.

Such a huge contrast to what he had been a moment ago. Like whatever batteries were charging him had died. Like he'd lost energy and power and had been forced to wait for someone to wind him up again.

And he looked at her.

And that look...

She would never forget that look.

It was a mixture of fear and pity.

And, although Cassy was too young to understand such a thing, it was a look of sorrow. Almost a look of apology.

And a look of hesitation.

The knock sounded again.

Wasn't he going to answer it?

But he didn't.

He just stood there.

Still.

Watching her. Staring. His lips pursed together, and his body slumped.

"Who is it?" Cassy asked, though her voice came out small.

He continued to stare at her.

Another knock, this time with a voice: "Charles, are you opening this door or not?"

His eyes closed. His face scrunched up. She swore she saw a tear appear at the top of his pale cheek.

"Don't tell me you wasted our fucking time again!"

Charles shook his head.

Cassy went to ask who it was again but didn't.

She was scared. He was acting so strangely, and she didn't like it.

"Charles," said another voice, this one sounding far deeper, far more authoritative. Strict, yet calm at the same time. "Open the door. If we have to pound it down, any deal is off."

He shook his head, shaking it more and more, as if he was

answering no to a question she hadn't heard, so vigorously, so eagerly despaired.

"I'm so sorry," he whispered to Cassy. "I am so, so sorry."

Cassy stood.

Something told her to stand. To get ready. That she would have to run.

But where to?

They were too high to jump out the window. There was one door. And these were adults.

"Really, I didn't want to have to do this."

Charles turned and scuttled like a beetle toward the door, then stopped again.

He turned over his shoulder.

"Really, I am."

She ran, disappearing around the corner, searching for somewhere to hide.

But where could she go where no one would find her?

She listened.

The front door opened and closed.

Muffled talking.

Charles spoke. Something like, "She's through here."

Steps pounded steadily closer.

A few of them. There were more people than the two voices she'd heard.

She ran.

From the room, across the corridor, into the bedroom. Into a wardrobe. She huddled into a ball, where she stayed. Crying silently and thinking of her Grandma. Of her Grandad.

How she wished they were there to protect her.

How she wished Sullivan had stayed.

How she wished he hadn't left her with this strange man.

It didn't take long until she heard the bedroom door open. It didn't take long until they found her.

SUTTON COLDFIELD, ENGLAND

CHAPTER THIRTY-TWO

PHILLIPE'S BREATH STUNK, AND SULLIVAN WASN'T WILLING TO smell it much longer.

"It is good that they left, Jay Sullivan," decided Phillipe. "It means we get to continue alone."

"If we are going to have this little date together, at least take off my blindfold so I can gaze lovingly into your eyes."

"You think you are funny, yes?"

"Is the Pope Catholic?"

Phillipe sighed.

Sullivan listened carefully to his steps. There were a few, then a slide. He'd turned around.

He probably stood there with his arms behind his back, being all thoughtful.

Sullivan had a few seconds. He had to do this quickly.

With his ankles bound to the chair, he pushed forward for leverage, putting pressure on his toes, building up his strength.

With a growl, he threw himself back, hard, landing with all the force he could manage upon a back already in pain.

The chair cracked, but it didn't smash.

He lunged himself upwards, threw himself back again and, sure enough, the chair became pieces of wood.

He freed his right hand from the rope, but the chair was still bound to his legs.

It was fine. He'd deal with that.

His next move was to swipe the blindfold off and look this psychopath in the face.

Phillipe was thin. Scrawny. His skin clung to his bones. His hair was short and black, parted and pressed to his head like a real-life imitation of Chucky.

Phillipe didn't waste his time. He lifted the hot iron rod he'd used to burn Sullivan's back and charged at him.

Sullivan grabbed Phillipe's wrist. The guy was weak and easy to overpower, but Sullivan's legs were still attached to pieces of chair. His movement was constricted. Phillipe was able to pull out a small blade and slice Sullivan's thigh. It hurt.

Phillipe stepped back, looking for other items on his table of tricks. It was a small, sliding metal table of instruments like a surgeon might use.

It was exactly as Sullivan expected.

"Come on, Phillipe," Sullivan said. "You're not a fighter. Your job is to torture. Not to out-muscle. You know you'll lose this fight."

Phillipe held the iron rod aloft and paused. Hesitated. Considered the truth in Sullivan's statement.

His body fell limp and he took a step back. He wasn't going to fight Sullivan – they both knew he wouldn't stand a chance.

This allowed Sullivan to leap onto his back again, this time slamming the chair down hard enough to break it and free himself completely.

He stood, brushing himself off, wincing from the pain on his back.

"Where are my clothes?" he asked.

Phillipe shrugged.

"No, really. Where are they?"

Phillipe pointed limply a bunch of clothes in the corner.

"Cheers."

Sullivan walked to his clothes and redressed, aware of Phillipe staring at him.

"You did a good job, by the way," Sullivan offered, slipping on his trousers.

"Oh, thank you." Phillipe smiled widely. This really seemed to brighten up his day.

"I've seen a lot of guys like you do their work. You really, really are something. Honestly."

"Thank you. Coming from someone such as yourself, that is really kind."

"Hugo will probably kill you when he finds out you let me go."

"Unlikely. Not many people can do what I can do."

Sullivan finished putting his top and shoes on and looked around.

"Right, I think I have everything. Good to meet you."

"Likewise."

With a smile, Sullivan walked past Phillipe to the stairs.

He entirely expected what happened next; which was why he was already holding his hand up to catch the iron rod as Phillipe swung it at his back.

"Really," Sullivan said. "That wasn't kind."

He held Phillipe's wrist, twisted the rod out of his grip, and took it for himself.

He struck it around Phillipe's face, ensuring to strike with the hot end.

Phillipe fell to the floor, and Sullivan struck him again.

"Please..." Phillipe pleaded. "I thought we respected each other..."

Sullivan raised an eyebrow, as if to say *really?* and pressed the hot end of the rod against Phillipe's throat. He held it there, allowing it to hiss. Phillipe squirmed, but Sullivan couldn't wait any longer. He had to go.

He had to get back to Cassy.

He dreaded to think of what might happen if Hugo got to her first.

CHAPTER THIRTY-THREE

HAD THEY REALLY FOUND CASSY? HOW HAD THEY FOUND her? Would Charles protect her? Was he even capable of protecting her?

So many questions, but none of them were helpful. All he could do was to get back to Cassy as quickly as possible. That would ensure he had the best chance. Nothing else mattered.

He swung open the door to the basement, ignoring the pain of his back. He burst into a corridor which led to more corridors. The route out of the building wasn't complicated, it just felt like it lasted forever.

He finally made his way into the open room of a warehouse. The exit was across the room.

He sprinted.

Ignoring the stitch.

Ignoring the fatigue.

Ignoring the searing pain of the burns on his back. It felt like he was still being tortured, like someone was flicking a hot elastic band against the same spot of his skin.

But it was skin. It would scab and heel. It wasn't like he needed to keep his body sacred for anybody. He ignored it as much as he could, refused to let the agony tamper with his judgement. He had to think clearly, however tough that was.

He used to be good at this.

He used to be *the best* at this.

And now he was battling the pains of aches, stitches and burns. He wondered how much his mind and body would be able to take.

"Shut up," he barked at his inner monologue. His mind and body would take whatever his mind and body had to take. This wasn't a time to ruminate on self-doubt.

He emerged into moonlight. He was in an industrial estate, but there was no one around. No people working, no trucks, no cars — and, most importantly, no vehicles to steal.

"Cassy..."

He listened. Intently. Carefully.

There was traffic. Nearby.

Where was it coming from?

He turned his head. It was coming from over his right shoulder.

He leapt over a fence and through a field of overgrown weeds. He emerged in another field, ran past a playground, and reached a road that wasn't too busy.

A man to his left was opening his car door, staring at his phone. Sullivan barged him out of the way.

"Hey!" shouted the man and lifted his arms to confront Sullivan. Sullivan easily took the stranger's wrist and twisted it behind his back. The stranger collapsed to his knees and whimpered under the pressure on his arm. Sullivan took the man's keys and mobile phone.

"I don't want to hurt you," Sullivan told him, and released him.

The man remained grounded as Sullivan stepped into his car, not daring to argue.

"I'm sorry," said Sullivan as he sped away.

He felt guilty. Not for the inconvenience for this man replacing a stolen car and stolen phone, or for the threat, but for the potential trauma. The man may just end up being more cautious, or it may affect him more deeply than that. Either way, Sullivan couldn't waste time on guilt.

He never had before.

He drove, looking for signs for the A38. Nothing.

Within a minute he reached a set of red traffic lights. This was annoying, but it gave him time to put *Aston* into the Google Maps app of the man's phone. Luckily, the guy hadn't had time to lock it. The location took a few seconds to appear. It was half an hour away. Sullivan hit *go*.

"Fuck that," he declared. He wasn't waiting half an hour.

He spun onto the wrong side of the road, overtaking the cars patiently waiting for a green light. Many cars had to break to avoid colliding with him, but he didn't care. He ignored the horns as he swung to the left and overtook another long set of cars.

He would not waste time on the highway code.

The Sat Nav said thirty minutes.

By overtaking cars and speeding, he reduced that to twenty-three.

He pulled into the car park of *The Queen's Nose,* and it didn't take him long to retrace his steps back to Charles' flat.

CHAPTER THIRTY-FOUR

Sullivan tried to open the door, but it was locked.

He kicked it. Again. And again, until the lock snapped, and the door swung against the inside wall.

He charged through.

Charles stood there idly. In the kitchen. By the window.

A face like a lost child.

"Where is she?" Sullivan asked.

Charles didn't answer. He turned away.

"Where is she?" Sullivan repeated, louder.

Still Charles didn't reply.

Sullivan didn't have time for his. He strode through the bedroom. To the bathroom. To the living room again.

At which point it dawned on him: she was not here.

"Do they have her?"

Charles looked away and closed his eyes.

Sullivan punched the wall, leaving a fist mark in the weak plaster.

"Charles?"

Charles went to open his mouth.

This was taking too long.

Sullivan grabbed Charles by the throat and dragged him to the sink.

Sullivan turned the hot tap. Let it run for a few seconds. Felt it getting hotter. And hotter. Until he couldn't keep his fingers under it any longer.

He put in the plug in held Charles' head, keeping the top of his head pressed against the base of the sink.

"Talk," Sullivan said.

The hot water sprinkled Charles' forehead, and he wept.

"It's too hot!"

"Then talk."

The water rose to cover his forehead. He wept and fidgeted, but Sullivan held him still.

"Do they have her?"

"Yes! Yes!"

Charles tried to move his head up, hoping it was over; but Sullivan was still not letting him move.

Sullivan was far from done.

He pushed Charles' harder, ensuring that not only would the hot water scald him, but the metal would grind against his skull.

"Why?"

"Because... They came..."

Charles wept and screamed. The water reached his eyes.

"How did they know she was here?"

No answer.

Just weeps.

So many damn weeps.

"How did they know? *How*?"

"I told them! I told them!"

Charles closed his eyes. The water reached his nose.

"Where are they going?"

"I don't know."

"You know Hugo Jones. Why would he want an eleven-year-old girl? Why?"

"I only know what I hear..."

"And what do you hear?"

"You are not going to like it, I–"

His mouth submerged.

Sullivan held Charles' head under the burning water just a moment longer. Long enough to show Charles that death was close. Enough to cease Charles' breathing and cause him as much distress as possible.

Sullivan pulled Charles out of the water and threw him to the floor. His face was red.

"Tell me," Sullivan demanded.

"Please–"

Sullivan kicked the heel of his shoe into the burns on Charles' cheek.

"You're wasting my time."

"They say... He takes them to some trucks... And the trucks take them..."

"Where are the trucks?"

"I don't know!"

Sullivan paced. Then halted. Paced again and halted once more.

He had no idea where to look for these trucks, but he knew where the trucks would take her. He had delved deep enough into the underworld in his time to know that, any time they put a child on a truck, the destination would not be a pretty one.

Most likely Eastern Europe.

A brothel.

Or something just as ugly.

He couldn't help thinking of Talia. Of his daughter. When she was taken by a man known for child trafficking, and the pain that caused him.

Charles furiously patted at his face. Crying. He should really get a cold flannel or something, but he wasn't daring to. Like there was an unspoken instruction that he was not allowed to ease his pain.

Like he didn't deserve it.

"Why?" asked Sullivan, his voice coming out differently to a moment ago. He had sounded so bold and determined, and now he appeared despaired and resolved.

He'd lost her.

He'd failed her.

And he'd let Connor and Elsie down.

They had taken him in.

And the one thing he was able to do, the *one damn thing*, was to kill and capture.

Now he could no longer do that.

"I thought he killed your wife. I thought the debt was settled."

"He said it still wasn't enough. He said I still owed him."

"So you saw this as an opportunity to get all square?"

Charles nodded. So feebly. Such a pathetic wreck of a man.

"And are you? All square, I mean? Is your debt settled?"

Charles nodded again.

"Well, I'm happy for you."

Sullivan stood. Anger spread throughout his body like wild-fire through a forest.

Charles would most likely get the brunt of it.

And Sullivan did not mind.

He did not mind at all.

In fact—

Wait...

Sullivan gasped.

"I know – I know where he's taking her."

Charles had said he takes them to some trucks.

Sullivan recalled the locations he had noted earlier: A warehouse. A home address. *An M6 service station.*

At the time, he'd thought a service station would be a stupid place to look...

But that would be it...

It must be...

"Get up," Sullivan said.

"What?"

"Get your car keys."

"But I–"

"You waste any of my time, I will kill you. Get me your keys."

Charles did as he was told.

CHAPTER THIRTY-FIVE

CHARLES SAT NERVOUSLY IN THE PASSENGER SEAT AS SULLIVAN drove. His face was in pain, and he felt humiliated to have been beaten up once again — though he'd grown used to the feeling of shame.

He had offered a child to the man who had murdered his wife — but it wasn't because of his debt, as he'd led Sullivan to believe. He had made a deal with Hugo for other reasons. And, whilst Sullivan recklessly negotiated the roads with no concern for the welfare of Charles' car, Charles thought back to the exchange he'd had in his flat just hours ago.

"Where are you taking her?" Charles had asked.

Hugo had looked back at him with the *are you kidding me?* look that intimidated Charles so much.

"Are you taking her overseas?" Charles asked.

One of Hugo's acquaintances carried the kicking and screaming girl over his shoulder and out of his flat.

"Wh – where are you taking her? Is she going where you take other girls? Are you leaving the country?"

No one reacted, even slightly, to Charles' questions.

"Please, let me come."

Hugo had let the others filter out, then paused, turning to Charles.

"Please."

He folded his arms, waiting dubiously for a decent reason he should help him.

"I appreciate that you consider the debt settled, I do. Really. It's just... my life here has been destroyed."

Hugo looked unsympathetic.

Charles was used to this, even from other criminals. There was a hierarchy amongst criminals, and, as a man who had been convicted for possession of child pornography, he was at the bottom.

There was no reason for Hugo to help him.

After all, last time Hugo had helped him escape prison time, Charles had entered the agreement knowing he hadn't the funds to pay for this favour. The one person who naively believed Charles was innocent, his wife, had paid the price.

"I'm on the register here. People find out who I am, and they don't want me. I can't leave the country as it breaks my parole. Barely a month goes by without my car being wrecked, or someone graffitiing on my door, and I–"

"I am waiting for the reason I should give a fuck."

"Because... you helped me before."

"Because I thought you could pay me for my help. I am not inclined to help paedophiles out of the goodness of my heart."

"I'm not a paedophile. I just made a mistake."

"We're settled. Don't let me see you again."

Hugo turned to leave.

"What if I deliver you the man too?"

Hugo paused.

"We have the man. He is being seen to."

"But–"

"Goodbye."

Then Hugo left. Charles had assumed the man was now dead — so imagine his surprise when the man had returned.

Charles hadn't a way to contact Hugo. He was hardly going to take his phone out and start texting.

But he hadn't needed to.

The man had somehow figured out where Hugo would take the girl; miraculously conjuring up a huge bit of luck.

From the moment Charles had seen them in the pub, talking about Hugo, he had felt it — these people were his salvation. Just imagine if he delivered the man to Hugo...

He could find somewhere abroad to start a new life. Establish himself under a new name. An alias. With people who didn't know his past. People who would have no chance of finding out.

People who wouldn't stare at him like he was scum.

But this man...

Charles watched him driving, his eyes on the road, speeding along the fast lane of the motorway. Any time he came up behind a car in the way of him, he would ride that car's bumper inches from collision until they moved over. He ignored the middle fingers and the shouts out of open windows. He didn't care.

Charles recognised the way the man was sweating from his days as a doctor working with alcoholics, and he kept clutching at his heart. After a bit of wincing, he took some pills out of his pocket and swallowed them dry.

"Did you want me to have a look at that?" Charles asked.

Sullivan said nothing. In fact, Charles was sure he heard a slight growl. He drove so close to a car in front Charles prepared for impact.

"Move," he grunted.

Eventually, the person moved out of the way, gesturing out of the window.

They passed a sign for the M6 service station, driving so quickly they almost missed it.

"What's your plan?" Charles asked.

Sullivan ignored him.

Everyone always ignored him.

He'd be angry if he wasn't so used to it.

"What can I do to help?" Charles persisted.

Sullivan swung across the middle lane and into the inside lane. He indicated left and pulled into the service station.

"I can help," Charles lied. "I can do something."

"The only thing you can do," the man said, "is stay still and shut up."

"But Hugo knows who I am. What if I go speak to him, tell him I need to show him something, lure him back here? How does that sound?"

CHAPTER THIRTY-SIX

Sullivan knew that, once Charles had located Hugo at the service station, he would undoubtedly tell Hugo where Sullivan was. He had been enough of an idiot to trust Charles once; he would not trust him again.

That he'd even trusted Charles in the first place was scary in itself – Sullivan's instinct had been that Charles was safe.

What did that say for his instincts?

What did that say for his abilities?

It wasn't just that his instinct was wrong; it was that he had relied on his instincts throughout his whole career. His gut told him when to proceed, when to wait, when to fight, and when to hide.

And, for the first time, his gut had betrayed him.

Nevertheless, he knew he would not find Hugo amongst this mass of trucks. There were too many to search. The truck would be indistinguishable from any other. The men would be inconspicuous; it wasn't like the movies where all the bad guys looked noticeably evil. You'd easily walk past a child trafficker in the street and have no idea.

Therefore, Sullivan had two options. Allow Charles to find

Hugo under the pretence of helping him then wait for the trap. Or, give Charles the chance to find Hugo and the truck, then find the truck by locating Charles.

Sullivan gave Charles a few minutes, then decided it was time to follow. He took the car keys out and paused.

Something moved out of the corner of his eye.

It might have been nothing, but considering the situation, it probably wasn't.

Something moved behind him.

He looked in the rear-view mirror.

A person ran from one bush to another. Holding a rifle. It happened in seconds, but he knew what he saw.

"Here we go."

Either he could get out of the car and run to cover now, or he could stay in the car and stay low; become a target they couldn't easily shoot from afar and force them to confront him at closer proximity. Sullivan's skill set was at its strongest in close proximity.

Before he had analysed the pros and cons, Charles reappeared. From beyond the trucks. With Hugo.

Charles pointed at Sullivan's car, and Hugo smiled at him. Patted him on the back. Nodded affirmatively.

Charles disappeared behind the trucks.

Sullivan imagined all the things he'd do to Charles should he ever get his hands on him. If they were ever reunited, he would ensure Charles would forever remember how he'd fucked him over.

For now, he had to think rationally.

Were they going for the kill, or for the capture?

Why would they not kill him? Why would they want to keep him? They have the information they needed. They had Cassy.

Sullivan had to assume they wanted him dead.

But no one had taken a shot yet.

Hugo was walking toward the car, grinning widely.

Sullivan looked through his surroundings. He saw the ends of rifles, people positioned beneath nearby trucks, behind bushes, a bench, more trucks.

"I assume you know we have you surrounded," Hugo declared.

Capture.

They were after the capture.

But why?

Unless someone else had put a contract on him. Could they be delivering him to someone?

Whilst there were many people who would want to kill him, he could not think of anyone other than the Falcons with the money or know-how to have put a price on his head in the last few days.

"Come out of the car with your hands in the air."

Someone must want him alive.

They must do.

He took the chance.

He complied. Stepped out, looking around. Two men behind a far bush. One behind a car. Another two behind Hugo

Sullivan put his hands in the air.

Hugo turned over his shoulder and called out. Moments later, a scrawny little man stepped out.

"What the..."

How on Earth had he survived?

Phillipe had marks on his face where Sullivan had struck him with the hot iron rod. A bandage around his neck where Sullivan had pressed the end of the rod against him. But he was alive and walking.

Phillipe nodded to Hugo and handed over an envelope of money.

Sullivan shook his head as he realised why he was alive. He knew men like Phillipe. They had egos that did not allow their victims to escape. They would not tolerate an incomplete job.

And that's exactly what Sullivan was.

"I take it we weren't done?" Sullivan said, unsure whether to rue or be grateful for Phillipe's ego keeping him temporarily alive.

Phillipe took a deep breath and strode quietly forward, placing each of his plaid shoes down carefully, not breaking his focus. He stopped inches from Sullivan's face.

"What's the matter?" Sullivan taunted. "Not used to people fighting back?"

"You may not understand what it is to be a professional anymore, Jay Sullivan, but a professional finishes his job."

Sullivan looked over Phillipe's shoulder to Hugo.

"I will give you whatever price you want for the girl," he said. "I will pay you ten times as much as he's paid you. Give me Cassy, and I will give you as much money as you ask for. Millions. I will disappear, and you will not hear from me again."

He waited for Hugo's response. He did not receive one.

"Come on," Sullivan said. "You will get more money from me than you would any buyer. Just let me take her."

"Again, Jay Sullivan," said Phillipe. "Trying to make one back out of a pre-arranged deal is ungentlemanly conduct. Let's remain professional."

Sullivan wanted to rip Phillipe's skinny little limbs from his body, tear him up, and force him to watch his own life end.

"You really are a fucked up little man, aren't you?"

Phillipe smiled. Chuckled.

"Taser him and put him in the boot of my car," he instructed.

Something hit his back. His muscles clenched. He fell. His arms felt like they would snap. It was like lightning going through his body.

His chest throbbed. It was making his heart condition worse. He needed his pills.

He tried to reach for them, only to find his arm unable to move.

Just as they lifted him into the boot of a car, he passed out.

CHAPTER THIRTY-SEVEN

THE SUN SHONE LIKE IT WAS THE CLICHÉ IN A HAPPY POEM.

Sullivan lay on the ground. His body wouldn't move. But his hands could.

Above him, she smiled.

He lifted his arm out to reach her. His hand passed straight through, like she was a ghost. Or a mirage. Or a hologram.

But she was there, he knew it.

Standing over him.

"Talia..." he whispered.

She did not reply. Just smiled back at him sweetly.

She was twelve. Which was strange, as he knew she would be nineteen now.

Even though it was strange, it was okay. He accepted it. Like one does.

She had that smile she had before everything fucked up. Back when he was still the world's biggest killer and back before he had ever lost her.

Back when he was far off being the pathetic fool he was now.

"Talia, what are you doing here?"

He sounded relieved.

Like she was the cure.

Like everything had ended, and it was okay again.

"I'm not," she said.

Even though she smiled, even though she ran her hand gently down her father's face, and even though the scene was of such beauty, there was a sadness in it.

Because she was right.

She wasn't really there.

And neither was Sullivan.

And soon, he would have to return to consciousness, and everything would be awful again.

Even though he knew it, he did not accept it.

No, this was his reality now. This was his truth.

She was still twelve. He was still a father. He was not a mess. She still loved him like a doting daughter would and she still wanted him around.

There was no Hugo. No Phillipe. No Charles.

But there was also no Cassy, and that ruined everything. Because that meant he hadn't saved her. He hadn't stopped her from suffering an abhorrent fate. An adolescence of abuse.

People don't recover from the kind of torture she was about to face.

And this meant he couldn't stay.

"Don't go," she said, her hand sliding into his like it was a mitten.

Sullivan shook his head. Closed his eyes so she wouldn't see tears. She'd never seen him sad. At least, not at that age.

That wasn't because he'd hidden sad moments; it was because he'd never been sad. He'd never felt much of anything but adoration for her. He was dead to anything else. But everything he was dead to had since become alive. And he felt guilt. Sadness. Regret. Remorse. Emptiness.

He had let Connor down.

Let Elsie down.

"You have to get her back, don't you?" she asked.

He nodded.

"Yes. I do."

"I wish you could stay here forever."

"So do I."

Oh, boy, so did he.

But she wasn't really staying in this lovely place; she was staying in his mind, and his mind wasn't a good place to be.

"Go," she said.

She stood, about to retreat to the back of his thoughts.

"I have to. I don't want–"

"I know."

She smiled another smile.

She looked so much like her mother.

"I love you," he said, but she'd already faded.

The sound of utensils against metal interrupted.

Drips.

Steps.

Every hair on end, rising to the cold of the room.

And his eyes were open.

And he was back again.

And Phillipe was standing over him.

CHAPTER THIRTY-EIGHT

HE NEEDED HIS PILLS.

They were in his jacket pocket.

Where was his jacket?

He looked to one side of the chair, to the other.

Nothing.

He was naked.

On a metal chair.

A *metal* chair.

That demented French sociopath stood over him, clicking the ends of what looked like medieval forceps.

There were three of him.

Blurry

Divided.

Shit, was he that delirious?

What had done that to him?

The taser? Concussion? Pills?

A mixture?

His faulty heart stung.

Normally a little twinge of pain in his chest meant it was time to take a pill. His chest was screaming.

Sullivan took a little comfort in knowing his heart would probably kill him before this bastard did. Without pills, he wouldn't last much longer.

Phillipe moved to behind Sullivan. Standing over the burn he had caused earlier.

He placed the end of his forceps against the edge of burn, gripping the burnt flesh, and pulled ever so slightly.

Sullivan shouted.

He didn't care.

He couldn't manage any more witty comments. Mental strength no longer fuelled perseverance. He could not out-think the pain.

He was exactly as Phillipe wanted him.

Phillipe continued prodding and peeling the burn — though he did not do so quickly. He moved slowly, leisurely; ensuring the pain was as drawn-out as possible.

It probably took minutes. To Sullivan, it took days.

He screamed out, only to hear his screams rebound back to him.

No one would hear him.

No one that cared, that was.

Phillipe strode to the front of Sullivan and dangled the forceps, exposing a piece of juice he'd extracted from the burn.

Phillipe found this hysterical.

The laughter entered Sullivan's mind like broken surround sound. The bass was turned up too high. The reverb was too long. It came from all angles, yet none at all.

He dropped his head, his eyelids wavering.

His heart was raging. Slowing. It would not beat much longer.

Sweet relief of death was close.

Only...

Cassy.

He'd let Connor down. He'd let Elsie down.

All he ever brought anyone was failure.

"No, no, no," Phillipe insisted, lifting Sullivan's head. "There will be no passing out, thank you. You are to stay awake for this."

Sullivan went to make some kind of witty comeback. Like, *you only ever stand a chance when I'm passed out,* or, *buy me dinner first, you demented bastard.*

All that came out was an empty stutter and a dribble of saliva.

"Oh, my," Phillipe said. "Icky."

Phillipe took a handkerchief and wiped the saliva from Sullivan's chin.

Sullivan attempted to bite at Phillipe's hand, who found this hilarious.

Phillipe took another utensil. It looked like a clamp. Rusty and hard.

Phillipe went to his knees. Crawled closer to Sullivan. Placed one side of the clamp beside Sullivan's left testicle. Placed the other next to Sullivan's right testicle. Looked up to Sullivan and grinned.

"Amateurs always neglect the genitals. Why attack someone's chest when you can destroy what really matters?"

He narrowed the ends of the clamp.

Sullivan stared helplessly as one of his testicles squashed against the other.

"This is for striking me with my own rod, Jay Sullivan."

Phillipe tightened again.

Then paused. A noise had distracted him.

A door opening and closing.

"Ah, putain de salaud!" he exclaimed, and stood, turning to see who was daring to interrupt.

A pair of high heels grew louder, and a woman walked in. A glamorous woman. Proud, well put together. Blank faced. Beautiful.

Sullivan recognised her.

Where did he recognise her from?

Hugo's wife.

"What is it?" demanded Phillipe.

"My husband is on the phone. He wishes to talk to you."

"Can you not tell him I am busy?"

She raised her eyebrows. "Would you ever tell my husband that the person he wishes to speak to is busy?"

Phillipe huffed.

"Where is the phone?"

"Upstairs. Bedroom."

Phillipe huffed again. "Why did you not bring it down?"

She smiled an intensely nasty smile.

"I guess I thought you needed the workout."

"Watch him," Phillipe demanded, pounding up the stairs, making his agitation clear.

The woman wasted no time. She rushed to Sullivan, diving to her knees, removing the clamp from his testicles. She pulled out a box of pills and poured them in her hand.

"How many?"

"Huh?" he said, too groggy to understand.

"How many pills do you need?"

"Er... two... three..."

She put three in his mouth.

"Swallow," she instructed.

He did as he was told.

She withdrew a knife and began cutting through the ropes.

Sullivan's heart still throbbed, but the pain lessened. Gradually. A small amount of clarity came back, and he realised she was helping him.

"What are you doing?" he asked.

Footsteps.

"Shit," she said. "He's coming back."

The door opened.

She placed the knife covertly into Sullivan's hand, concealing it behind the chair, and quickly placed the testicle clamp back where it had been.

"What are you doing?"

"I didn't have enough time," she whispered in Sullivan's ear. Steps came down the stairs. "Meet me in the car outside. Hurry."

She stood.

"What are you doing?" asked Phillipe, reaching the bottom step.

"I was just having a little word with him," she said. "Telling him what a fool he is for trying to fuck with a man like my husband."

"Well, there was no phone call."

"There was. I left the phone on the—"

"If you don't mind, I would appreciate some privacy."

She looked to Sullivan, who looked weakly back up at her.

He could think again.

His body was still in agony. His mind was heavy. His back throbbed and burnt. He was too fatigued to endure the pain. But at least his heart had stopped killing him.

He was already working his way through the ropes binding his wrists, keeping his arm movements still to avoid giving away what he was doing.

She nodded to Phillipe. Walked up the stairs. Looked back before she left, glancing once more at Sullivan.

She shut the door behind her.

"Right," said Phillipe, returning to his knees and taking hold of the clamp. "Where were we?"

CHAPTER THIRTY-NINE

Phillipe placed a hand either side of the clamp.

He grinned.

He'd noticed how many other torturers would continually punch the victim's face or stab their chest. It was silly. They never focussed on the one thing a man would truly hate to lose: his cock.

Phillipe always used the cock as a big finale. With Sullivan, however, he was desperate to inflict pain, too eager to show that no one *ever* escaped him, that he decided to go straight to the big finish. Ready to crush and mangle and contort and do everything a man would dread happening.

Often, Phillipe wouldn't even have to start this part of the torture. He would place the clamp by a testicle, and the victim would be willing to tell you everything from secret codes to the colour of his wife's thong.

He tightened the clamp. Sullivan winced.

He grinned because it excited him. Not a sexual thrill. Just simple satisfaction for the pain he was about to cause.

Especially to this over-hyped former legend.

Everyone had always spoken of him in such high regard.

They said he could not be killed. That he was invincible. That he had mastered the art of murder.

It was sacrilege.

Phillipe had mastered the art of murder, not this charlatan.

An assassin could never do what he did. His work was a thing of beauty. A passion. Sullivan's work was a job.

He tightened the clamp further. Sullivan's testicles pressed together, one atop the other like they were climbing into a tiny bunk bed.

He readied his arms for the big push, preparing for a large swing, ready to slam the clamp together and watch them burst.

Ready to–

"Aaaargh!"

Sullivan's arms, liberated from the rope, lifted into the air.

How the fuck did he do that? Phillipe was an expert at knots. No one could untie a rope when he'd bound it. No one could...

A knife.

Sullivan raised a knife into the air.

What an idiot Phillipe was.

Of course, the woman would betray her husband.

Of course, she would give him the knife.

Just as Phillipe went to swing his arms into the clamp, hoping to have his final bit of fun before Sullivan did, the bastard plunged the knife into his shoulder.

Phillipe fell back and writhed in pain.

Sullivan discarded the clamp and attempted to stand, but fell.

He dragged himself across the floor and to the stairs, using the bannister to pull his battered body upwards.

He forced his legs to move; demanded that they work. Despite being numb, he managed to balance precariously upon them.

As Phillipe lay there, bleeding profusely, Sullivan found his way out of the house.

Leaving Phillipe on the floor of the basement.

Leaving Phillipe to sit up and grab a towel.

Leaving Phillipe to rue his own stupidity.

But, unbeknownst to Sullivan – leaving Phillipe alive.

CHAPTER FORTY

HE CRAWLED INTO THE BACK OF THE CAR WITHOUT A WORD or question. Hugo's wife was behind the wheel and, as soon as Sullivan was in, she took off.

He said nothing.

Didn't ask what she was doing. Why she was doing it. He just lay upon the backseat, allowing the ache to overcome him.

"There are clothes there for you," she said. "And a bandage.

He retrieved the bandage first, and wrapped it around his torso, covering the wound Phillipe had left upon his back, flinching at the pain. He knew he should clean it to ensure it did not get infected, but he hadn't the energy — the bandage would do.

He half-heartedly dragged the underwear and suit trousers over his lower half. He shoved his arms through the shirt and did enough buttons up to conceal part of his chest, cursing again at the pain on his back. There was a suit jacket that he also pulled on. It was tight, but he preferred a slim fit suit.

He always looked better in a slim fit.

But, even now, it felt like the suit over his body was the reason the phrase *polished turd* had ever been invented. He usually felt better in a suit, yet this was not having the redeeming effect he had hoped for.

His body flopped. His eyelids tried to close.

He rotated his head and slumped it to the side, looking at the back of the woman's head.

Her hair was pulled back into a ponytail. Her neck was smooth. Not even a dimple. Even in his absent state, he could see her clothes were expensive. They were fashionable, but not fashionable in the way teenagers were fashionable; this was not a woman who would wear ripped jeans. Her clothes were fashionable in the way that a woman who was rich and well-kept would be fashionable.

"Well," Sullivan said, his voice coming out as a croak. "You've seen me naked now. You can at least tell me your name."

She turned a corner and glanced at him in the rear-view mirror.

"Charlene."

"Charlene," he repeated. "What's going on, Charlene?"

"I know who you are."

Her sentence took a while to make sense. How tired was he?

"You are Jay Sullivan," she continued. "You are a great assassin."

"*Was* a great assassin, Charlene. Now I'm the world's greatest failure."

"I don't believe that. A man like you doesn't just lose all his ability."

"Watch me."

He stretched his back and winced. He lay back down, closed his eyes, and reminded himself of his motivation.

Cassy.

"I need to go. I need to get to—"

"The truck with the girl in. I know."

"Then what are–"

"We are going there now."

He huffed. He knew this wasn't confusing, but he was exhausted. His body was shaking, and he was struggling to make sense of anything.

"Get some sleep," she told him. "It's a long journey. We can talk when you wake up."

"But..."

"The truck is taking off on a ship in Southampton. We have at least three hours, and that's if I drive quickly. Sleep."

He had no choice but to take her advice. He had been awake for over fifty hours. Without rest, he would be reckless.

So, against his better judgement, he allowed his eyes to close and fell into a heavy sleep.

CHAPTER FORTY-ONE

CASSY SHIVERED.

The darkness made it colder.

She was wearing just a t-shirt and leggings.

Was it night-time?

Or was it just that they had concealed the light?

She rubbed her arms. Her whole body shook. She had goose bumps. She was hyperventilating.

Was she shivering because she was cold or scared?

She wished she was somewhere else. Anywhere else.

Where had Sullivan gone?

Where had that Charles man gone?

She could tell the truck was moving. The jitters of an engine rumbled her body.

She tucked her arms around her legs, holding her knees tight to her chin.

There was sobbing. It was faint. There were a lot of girls in the truck with her. She'd seen at least a dozen others before the doors were closed and the light had been stolen.

Everyone stayed in their own space. No one dared invade another's.

Had they all been taken too?

The silence was miserable. Like they were too afraid to cry. Like they didn't want to be heard. Crying was a burden. A weakness. What would their captors do if they heard it?

Who even were their captors?

Where was she going?

What was happening?

She closed her eyes.

She was back on the farm.

Grandad had tucked her in the previous night, and now he was opening the curtains and telling her breakfast would be ready soon.

She was skipping downstairs. There was bacon. Scrambled egg. Cheesy toast. Grandma was already halfway through hers.

She said they were going to town that afternoon.

That meant she had the morning to herself.

She played on the swing set and she pushed herself so high that her legs blocked the sun.

She kicked the ball against the wall.

Then she played her guitar. For hours. Did the exercises Sullivan had taught her. Played *Twinkle Twinkle*.

Grandma took her to town.

She had a cream doughnut in her Grandma's favourite café. The café was owned by a friend her Grandma used to go to school with. Every time Cassy went in there, that friend would say to her, "Do you know I went to school with your Grandma? She was quite the rascal!"

She heard it every time, but she never grew tired of it. She liked to imagine her Grandma as a young girl, her age, up to mischief.

When she arrived home again, Grandad would give her a big hug and told her he missed her. She would say she missed him too. Because she did.

She missed him a lot.

She stretched her arms out as her memories faded, as if her fingertips could hold on to them. As if she could stop them from leaving.

But they were already gone.

She was just remembering memories.

She'd never have those memories again, not since those men ki–

She closed her eyes. She couldn't think it.

Someone was sobbing loudly. Crying hard, as if they had just woken up and realised where they were. Quickly, those cries turned into screams. The girl was pounding against the walls, crying out in a language Cassy didn't recognise.

A bang came from the cab.

"Knock it off!" said a voice. Gruff, deep, booming.

The girl did not stop. She continued to bang, to scream, to cry out.

"I said fucking knock it off!"

The girl screamed even harder.

The cab opened. A man crawled through the space. The light behind him exposed the tattoos on his neck, and on his knuckles. His hair was greasy, and his body was big.

He charged toward the crying woman and grabbed her by the hair.

She cried out.

He drove her head into the side the wall of the truck.

She whimpered.

He did it again.

The girl still cried. Still screamed. Still made far too much noise that was sensible.

The man took a gun from his back, aimed it at her head, and shot.

The crying and screaming stopped.

He turned and looked at the rest of the girls.

"Bud'-khto inshyy?" he asked.

Although Cassy couldn't understand him, she knew not to answer.

He returned to the front of the truck. He and someone else laughed. They closed the cab, and the girls returned to darkness.

Cassy stayed still, aware that a dead body lay just metres from her.

No one dared to scream again.

CALIFORNIA, UNITED STATES

CHAPTER FORTY-TWO

THE MOTHER SHIELDED HER SON AND DAUGHTER.

"Leave us alone!"

She screamed so hard her voice gave out and she bellowed nothing but empty air.

"You will not hurt them!"

It was Jay Sullivan's mission.

He had to do his mission.

It didn't matter who they were.

It didn't matter.

He had to do it.

He had to.

Except, the memory was skewed. This wasn't what had actually happened. This was his memory haunting his sleep, and sleep has a way of twisting reality.

He had been calm and professional when he'd performed this hit, but that wasn't how he was recalling it. He didn't stand strong as he had before. He wasn't void of emotion. Tears crept down his cheeks. The hand holding out the knife was wavering. Shaking.

"Please don't do this," he said to himself.

This was lasting longer than the actual hit had. The mother and children should be dead by now. But he didn't want to kill them anymore. He didn't want anyone to be dead because of him.

He pulled on his arm, tried to hold it back as it hacked away at the mother and slit the throat of the boy.

Then the girl looked at him.

Big eyes. Little face. Sadness in her cheeks.

It was the face of Cassy.

The girl he wished to save.

As if changing one girl's fate would have any bearing on the evil he had committed. Like stopping one girl from being trafficked would give him any kind of restitution.

"I'm sorry," he told her, his voice shaking. "I'm sorry I'm a bad man."

Cassy stood.

Placed her gentle palm on his knife hand. Pointed it toward her.

She didn't fight it.

She didn't seem lost. Sad. Or scared.

She was helping him do it.

But he didn't want to.

He was aware this was a memory. And he knew that, in this memory, he murdered the girl.

But he didn't want to murder her.

And he didn't want to hurt Cassy.

"Do it," she told him.

"No! No, I will not! I am not that person!"

But he was that person.

No amount of protestation would change the things he'd done.

Did he think this ridiculous, hopeless pursuit of a wayward child mattered? Did he really think that? Did he really think his half-hearted attempt to save Cassy would change anything about who he was, or what he'd done?

He'd have to kill more people to save her. So what if he'd be killing people more deserving of such a fate? He'd still be killing people.

All he offered this girl was more death.

And that was what she was asking for.

Sullivan didn't want to live, but the one life he knew was right to take; his own — that action evaded him.

He fell to his knees.

Buried his head in his hands.

Pretended this had never happened.

Eventually, the dream left, and empty sleep resumed.

THE A36, ENGLAND

CHAPTER FORTY-THREE

Sullivan awoke. His head pounded.

He knew he'd been dreaming.

But it was only a dream, that was all. Yet, as he felt relief it was just a dream, he remembered that the memory within the dream was real.

He leant up, rubbing his forehead.

"There are painkillers in the back of the chair," said Charlene.

It took him a moment to remember who she was and what had happened. He searched the back of the chair and found a packet of painkillers.

It might be poison. But it wouldn't make sense for her to rescue him from torturous death, give him medication to save him, and not kill him in his sleep.

He took two pills and crawled over the gear stick, into the passenger seat.

His suit was scruffy. One should never wear a good suit badly; it was practically sacrilege. He tucked the shirt in. Buttoned the rest of the bottoms, bar the top one. Straightened the collar of the blazer.

He finally turned and had a good look at the woman beside him.

Wow. She was a knockout. The perfect picture of a trophy wife. Slim. Slick. Seductive. Everything about her oozed sensuality. From the cut of her skirt to the fit of her jacket to the bounce of her hair.

He grew excited just looking at her. What he'd give for the touch of a woman like that.

He shook his head. All he had to do was look at a pretty woman and he'd fall in love. Was that how lonely he was — that some menial attention from the opposite sex, not at all sexual, was enough to convince him of eternal adoration? So pathetic.

He had to remind himself that she was Hugo Jones' wife. Why on earth was she helping him?

He looked out of the window. They passed a sign for Salisbury. This was the A36. They must be half an hour away now, give or take.

"How long have I been out?" he grumbled.

"Just over three hours. You were talking in your sleep."

"Was I?"

"Do you normally talk in your sleep?"

"Don't know. Been a while since I've had someone around to tell me."

"Then I am honoured to be such a person."

He looked at her curiously. Was she flirting with him?

"What's your deal?" he asked.

"Excuse me?"

"If Hugo is your husband, I'd imagine helping me will not do you any favours."

"I hate my husband."

"Every wife hates their husband. Why are you doing this?"

She hesitated. Her playful demeanour dropped.

"He killed our son," she said.

"Your son?"

"Nathaniel."

"Nathaniel, why do I remember—"

He paused. Thought. He had definitely heard someone refer to Nathaniel...

Connor.

The man who had helped Connor and disappeared. The reason he was short of staff.

Shit.

That's why they went after Connor and his family...

In a way, Sullivan was relieved. It meant their deaths weren't his fault. They would have happened anyway, and no one would be trying to rescue Cassy.

Then he felt ashamed for his relief and resumed his feeling of guilt.

"That's pretty harsh," said Sullivan.

"Harsh? Is that what you call it?"

She was scary when she was angry.

"Why'd he do it?"

"He believed Nathaniel to be a snitch. That he was talking to the police."

"And was he?"

"I stay out of my husband's affairs. I do not care to ask. The only thing I know is that Hugo demands true loyalty, from everyone. Including his son."

"Including you."

This seemed to make her smile again.

"That's why you need to kill him."

"Excuse me?"

"This is the deal I'm offering you. I show you where to find the girl you are after. In return, you kill my husband."

"How did you know I was after the girl? Thought you don't mess with your husband's affairs?"

"That was before he murdered my son."

Sullivan took a big breath.

His brain felt like it was expanding against his skull. He found a bottle of water by his feet. Without caring how long it had been there, he unscrewed the top and gulped down the entire contents.

He watched Charlene as she drove.

She made him think of Stacey.

If Stacey had known about Grant's real occupation, would she have reacted like Charlene?

No, of course not. Stacey was too rational. Too shy. She was always the one to bring some clear thoughts to a situation.

He regretted the way he'd left it with Stacey. He wished he could explain more. Maybe if he had the opportunity, he'd try again. He owed it to her and Grant.

They passed a sign for Southampton. Twenty miles.

"What if the ship isn't there?" Sullivan asked. "What if we've missed it?"

She smiled.

A cheeky smile.

A smile that made his entire body tingle.

He did not know what it was, but there was something about this woman that gripped him. Everything about her was sex. She practically defined the word.

"It's a shame," he said.

"What?"

"That you married such an animal."

"Why's that, Mr Sullivan? You think you'd have made an honest woman out of me?"

He turned and looked out of the window.

He was in love once. Had a family. Had a daughter.

That was before his wife's murder, almost two decades ago.

Jesus, has it been that long?

And, in all that time, he had only been intimate with hookers and sluts. Never anything meaningful. Never willing to fall in love for fear of putting someone in the firing line.

"What's the matter?" she asked. "Did I touch a nerve?"

"I don't think it's sensible to get involved with me, Charlene."

"I'm a big girl."

"And I think you will be thoroughly disappointed."

"Why? Don't think you can keep up with me?"

"I mean with me. As a person. As an assassin. I am nothing like I once was."

She smiled at him and his heart beat that little bit faster.

"I think you underestimate yourself, Mr Sullivan."

"Call me Jay."

"I think you underestimate yourself, *Jay*."

The way she said Jay with that whisper and pout... If silk could talk, her voice was how it would sound.

He said nothing more, and she seemed to be okay with that.

It didn't take much longer until they arrived at the dock to find that the ship had already left.

SOUTHAMPTON, ENGLAND

CHAPTER FORTY-FOUR

Sullivan kicked a crate of boxes across the dock.

"You are fucking kidding me!" he barked.

A group of tourists shuffled past.

"What?"

They ran on.

Charlene stood by the car. Watched him.

He turned and glared at her.

She was still smiling.

"What? What are you so smug about? Are we even at the right place?"

She walked forward and went to speak.

He interrupted her by kicking another crate, then bemoaned the pain in his foot.

She placed a hand on his shoulder. It felt good, and he told himself to stop liking it.

"Jay," she said.

"What?"

"I know where he's going."

"Where?"

"Odessa. In Ukraine."

"And what bloody good does that do us now? What, are we going to get to the airport in time for a plane? By the time we get there, they'll have gone and we'll have no fucking idea!"

She smiled again. Why did she keep smiling?

"Let me explain to you how my husband's business works. He owns a transportation business, which acts as a cover for transporting of goods to Ukraine. He always prefers to go by boat so he can keep all the trucks together — which means the journey will take him four days. Well, four days and eight hours to be precise. Do you know how long it will take us to drive to Ukraine?"

It didn't take Sullivan long to come up with an estimate. He'd travelled the world enough.

"About forty-eight hours if we don't stop."

"Which means we have enough time to get through the channel tunnel, have a sleep on our journey, and still make it to Odessa first."

"If you're lying to me, Charlene – if any of this is bullshit–"

She placed a hand in Sullivan's.

"He killed my son," Charlene said and, in her next breath, added, "Let's go; I want to be there waiting for him."

Sullivan looked over her shoulder at her car.

"We'll need to get a rental car; your husband will probably recognise that car. We can't risk anything."

"As you wish."

Within an hour they had acquired a rental car and were on their way to Kent. Sullivan insisted that Charlene rest for the first part of the journey, but really it was so he could ensure they took the correct route. Not that he didn't trust her; it was that too many people had already deceived him.

Once they had made it through the Channel Tunnel, had crossed France and passed through Belgium, he would be fine.

As it was, Charlene fell asleep and Sullivan kept driving. He drove through the Netherlands and into Germany, only waking Charlene when she needed to show her passport.

It was the next morning by the time he stopped at a motel just outside of Berlin and woke her up.

BERLIN, GERMANY

CHAPTER FORTY-FIVE

Sullivan was growing tired, so allowed Charlene to do the talking. She bought them a room for the night and paid in cash.

As they approached the room, Sullivan considered what to do with the downtime. It felt wrong to be doing nothing, but they were days ahead of Hugo. Maybe he could shop for a new suit or two.

Before he did anything, however, he had to talk to Stacey again. He'd made the decision while he was driving. He hated the way he left things with her, and he hated what she now thought of her husband. He had to find a way to explain it to her.

"Hey, do you mind if I borrow your phone?" Sullivan asked.

"Sure, I'll get it for you once we're in the room."

They entered the room. Sullivan halted.

"What is this?" he asked.

"What's what?" she answered.

"This." Sullivan waved his arm to indicate that there was one double bed, and nothing else. "Did you not ask for a twin room?"

She dropped her bag and turned to him, smiling in that sultry way he imagined had made Hugo go weak for many years. She moved closer, placing her soft hands over his coarse fingers.

"And won't your husband be pissed off?"

It was a ridiculous question and Sullivan was bemused at himself for asking it. It wasn't that he cared about hurting Hugo, of course he didn't — it was that this didn't feel right.

Still, that had never stopped him before. Why turn down a beautiful woman offering herself to him?

But that wasn't who he was anymore. Or, at least, it wasn't who he wanted to be. He was trying to be a good person, even if he wasn't exactly sure what being a good person meant.

"Exactly," she answered, putting her fingers through the back of his hair and whispering softly against his ear. "It will make him angry, and that is the reason we should do it."

"I can't."

"Oh, come on, we both know–"

"Please, can I just borrow your pho–"

She put both of her hands behind his head, grabbed him, and pulled him close, pressing her lips against his. He initially did nothing. It was hard to stop her — this wasn't a small, unassuming kiss; it was fiery and passionate. She was pressing her lips so hard it hurt. Her hands were running all over his body, grabbing and clutching at him.

They had a few hours to kill, but not like this. A little girl was missing. It wasn't right.

He pushed her off.

"No," he said.

"Are you kidding?"

He said nothing.

"Come on, it won't–"

"Just give me your phone."

Reluctantly, she took out her phone and handed it to him.

Her face was disgusted. As if it was an unusual, bizarre occurrence for a man to turn her down.

Sullivan couldn't believe he was actually turning her down. Everything in his body was screaming at him to move closer, to just go with her.

But he had a bit of spare time, and there was a phone call he had to try making. He had to do the right thing, as uncharacteristic as that was.

He walked out of the room, leaving her to her defiant arousal.

CHAPTER FORTY-SIX

SULLIVAN STOOD AT THE EDGE OF THE CAR PARK. CHARLENE'S silhouette moved behind the curtains of their room. Even the way her shadow moved was angry.

He looked at the phone.

He planned out what he would say. How he would explain it. How he would undo a life of lies and make it all make sense.

This would be noble. This would be a good thing he did. For once, he would do a good thing.

He dialled the number. Waited. Felt suddenly nervous.

He told himself to stop it. Grant had been a good friend, and Sullivan didn't have many of them. He had to do right by him.

You can end a career as a killer, but it will catch up with you at some point, and it will not let you go. You are never free. You are never released of the recurring images of what you've done.

He had to make her understand.

He could be dead at any moment. It was hardly a safe mission to ambush a group of armed men, especially on a boat where there was no escape. Once upon a time he wouldn't have even entertained the possibility of his own death; now it seemed imminent. This may be the only chance he had to explain things to her.

Following a short period of silence, a computerised woman's voice spoke down the phone.

"All unrecognised numbers to this phone have been blocked. Please contact the–"

"Fuck!"

Sullivan dropped the phone. Punched the nearest car. Growled.

Stacey had blocked all unrecognised numbers. There was no way to talk to her.

Some strangers looked at him, but he didn't care.

Stacey would believe he and Grant were killers. That was what she wanted. To stubbornly assert her preconceived notions of what they were.

Grant was a killer.

Sullivan was a killer.

Evil was all they would ever be.

Hell, maybe she was right. Maybe he was just a murderer, nothing else. Death was all he offered, and that was not what Stacey wanted.

Stacey was probably right to stop him from calling. She was probably right about everything.

He bowed his head. He couldn't think. His belly churned. Rage gripped his body.

He saw Charlene again. In the room. Alone.

Charlene, who wanted him.

Charlene, who was probably the only person who was aware of the kind of things he'd done and still spoke to him like he was human.

He strode through the car park, pushed the door open, and stood there glaring at her.

"What is it?" Charlene asked as he approached.

He wanted to thrash out. Kill something. Punch someone. He wanted to do anything to channel this fury. And there she was, a simple release. Just the scent of her seemed to quell it.

"Come on," Charlene said. She put a gentle hand on his arm and leant into his chest.

"You married one killer, why do you want to fuck another? What is wrong with you?"

She didn't falter. Didn't crack. Her smile remained.

She leant in close and spoke quietly.

"You are not a killer," she told him.

"Then you can't know what I've—"

"I know killers," she said. "I know a lot of them. I am surrounded by my husband's men; all I do is speak to killers. You are *not* one of them."

He watched her.

She watched back.

So beautiful. So full of lies.

Whether or not she meant what she said, it filled him with a lighter sense of being. It lifted his burdens.

She was an escape.

And oh, how much he wanted that escape.

He longed to be inside of her, to feel the body that believed he could be good.

He longed to pretend she was right.

He needed to shove his anger into her, to grab her, to throw her, to...

He thrust his lips against hers.

She kissed back just as hard. Threw him to the rough carpet. The burn on his back stung like a bitch, but he ignored it. His jacket was off and his shirt was off and his trousers were around his ankles and she was taking off her bra and she was on top of him — and all of this happened before he fully comprehended it was happening.

She pressed her hands against his chest, grinding, gripping

him, moaning, lifting her head back, pointing perfect breasts to the sky.

She leant back and grabbed his shins, stretching, moving her hips, forcing him further inside of her. He tried moving, tried to join in, but she threw her arms against his chest, held him still, and moved harder.

She shoved her mouth against his so hard it hurt. She bit his lip, and he tasted blood.

She screamed. Sullivan feared that someone may hear them and come and enquire what they were doing.

No one did.

She rode him harder and harder until her screams became too much and he came and she came and he did nothing but lay there, staring up at this gorgeous, naked, fucking perfect specimen sitting on top of him.

They stayed like this. Panting. Staring.

Their breathing subsided.

She was smiling. A naughty smile. A kinky, fucked-up little slant in the corner of her mouth.

"You don't need to take more pills for your heart now, do you?" she whispered; though God knows why she was whispering — her screaming could probably have been heard all around the motel.

"After that? I think I'm going to need a few."

She laughed. Rested her head against his. And they kissed. Softly, this time. More affectionate. And he almost forgot that he was a loser who'd killed hundreds of people, trying to find a lost girl.

Then he remembered, and, as he looked at her, his smile faded, as did hers in return.

"What is it?"

He said nothing, but it all came back. This all suddenly felt so wrong.

Her dead son.

A girl being trafficked.

Who was he to have this kind of pleasure?

"It's okay," she told him.

She lay by his side, took his head, and held it to her chest, stroking his hair.

"It's okay," she kept whispering. "It's okay."

And, although it wasn't okay, he allowed himself, for a moment, to feel like he wasn't alone.

If he could have ever cried, it would have been then.

Fortunately, he did not allow himself such a pleasure.

THE NORTH ATLANTIC OCEAN

CHAPTER FORTY-SEVEN

SALVATION ISN'T ALWAYS WORTH SALVAGING.

It was a ridiculous saying Charles' grandmother used to say, and he always used to think she was nuts. It wasn't a phrase he'd heard from a movie, or literature, or anything. She just liked to invent and declare sayings as she sat proudly in her armchair. As if she could produce profound revelations out of the deteriorating intelligence of her mind.

But, as Charles sat aboard the ship, watching as Hugo's thugs and lackeys paraded cockily around the deck, he contemplated the phrase.

They were all patting each other on the back for a job well done. Hugo was smoking a cigar, and everyone was grinning.

They got the girls!

They left the UK!

They were setting sail for the Atlantic Ocean with no one to stop them!

There would be no way that the police wouldn't be aware that a truckload of girls had just left for Eastern Europe. It wasn't just girls, either — the vehicle deck was full of trucks transporting various illegal items.

But Hugo had enough money that it didn't matter.

In fact, he was evidence of just what money could buy. A trophy wife. Dozens of mistresses across different countries. A group of obedient bitches doing his work.

But mostly, fear.

Fear that meant judges wouldn't agree to search warrants. That meant prosecutors wouldn't prosecute. That meant police wouldn't press charges.

His money would pay for the death of the family of anyone who dared.

Charles considered himself to be a victim of the fear Hugo incited. The man had killed his wife for Christ's sake! And here he was, still asking Hugo for help. His wife had been the only person who had believed Charles' innocence when he was charged with his offences. Foolishly so, yes, as he was guilty — but that was how much she loved him. How much she doted on him. No amount of evidence, not even a confession, would convince her he wasn't a good man.

He had explained the possession of child pornography as a glitch. A temporary moment of madness. Hugo's money had saved him from prison. And his debt to Hugo had lost him the one person who still spoke to him.

There were no family members ready to talk to him. No friends. Neighbours campaigned for him to be removed from their neighbourhood. His brothers and sisters didn't want to know.

Without his wife, he was truly alone.

Yet, here he was, onboard a ship with the man who had sanctioned that murder, having begged for his aid. And, to add an even fouler taste to his mouth, he had done so at the expense of a young girl, and the man trying to save her.

That new life their sacrifice had given him was his salvation. Yet, somehow, it didn't seem so sweet. It seemed tainted. Like he didn't deserve it.

Not just because of his actions, but because of who he was.

He detested himself.

He was a loner. A weirdo. A bumbling fool.

The kind of man who would drop something and no one would help.

The kind of man who would apologise to someone who had punched him for hurting their fist.

The kind of man who would solicit the person who killed his wife for help.

That girl. Cassy. She was on the vehicle deck. In a truck.

The man was probably dead. Charles had handed him over like money to a butcher.

He bowed his head. Rubbed his sinus. He had a migraine. But he didn't take paracetamol.

He deserved the migraine.

He deserved more than the migraine.

He stood. It was a sudden movement, one he wasn't even aware of himself, but he did it nonetheless.

He wandered through the ship, to the stairs, and descended the steps.

What was he doing?

Stop it. You're a coward, accept it.

Except he wouldn't. Not this time.

No matter what happened to him, whether it be death or torture, for once he would do the right thing.

He would let those girls out.

There must be an emergency lifeboat or something. They could escape on that.

He would go down to the vehicle deck and he would open the door and out they would run.

They would thank him.

Cassy would exonerate him. Would say he finally did the right thing.

But he just had to open the door to the vehicle deck below just slightly to realise he would do no such thing.

The truck was quite a few vehicles down. Many big, beefy men surrounded it.

One of them reached into his jacket pocket, and the jacket moved enough to reveal a concealed gun.

Who was Charles kidding?

He would not do the right thing.

He wasn't even going to do a thing.

He would sit upstairs, watch the man who murdered his wife celebrate, and do nothing. Besmirching his wife's memory with lethargy.

He dropped his head. Plodded up the stairs at a far slower pace than he had descended them.

Sorry, Cassy.

He was just pretending.

There would be no one saving her today.

BERLIN, GERMANY

CHAPTER FORTY-EIGHT

WITHIN MINUTES, IT LOOKED LIKE CHARLENE HAD NEVER had sex at all.

That ravenous sexual appetite, the carnal lust Sullivan had gripped onto with his sweaty fingers, that dominance that overcame him was gone.

She looked into the mirror and sorted herself out. Straightened her jacket. Her top. Her hair.

Fuck, you are beautiful, Sullivan went to say.

But didn't.

It just didn't feel right.

He was still laid on the carpet of the motel room, naked, and with the remnants of sex sticking to his belly.

She had smartened herself up again. However much Sullivan admired this manufactured beauty, he had admired the carnal beauty far more.

She leant against a table and smiled at him. A knowing smile. An infectious smile. One that briefly prompted a twinge in the corner of his mouth.

"You're always so serious," she said.

He looked away.

"Even now," she continued, "after we have had sex, and pretty brilliant sex, you won't even smile. You won't even let yourself be happy, even for a moment. Will you?"

And there was the question.

The one any prospective woman always has to ask.

Why is he so fucking miserable?

He stood. Hobbled to the bathroom. Took some toilet paper and cleaned himself up, then pissed.

"No answer?" she said as he walked out.

"What do you want me to say?" he asked.

"Is there something you're grateful for, at least?"

He locked eyes with her.

"Not a thing."

"You don't even–"

"Cassy is still there. On that ship. On that truck. Probably going to some brothel where, if I don't find her, she'll be stuck. And– and–"

"And why is it your responsibility?"

He looked at her and scoffed.

"You really don't have a conscience, do you? Course not. You married Birmingham's biggest gangster."

"I married for love."

"Yeah, and how did that work out?"

"Poorly. But I'm hoping the next one will be better."

She leant toward him with that slight smile, that sexy glint, and kissed him. He let her, but did not kiss back.

"If you're implying that the next one will be me, you're barking up the wrong tree, lady."

"Look, I get it, everything is shit, you lost a lot, you want to live your life in exile, blah blah blah. But what if you don't have to be some nameless nobody?"

"Is that what I am? Some nameless nobody?"

"I'd like to find out."

"All I care about is getting that girl and getting her out."

"What about the other girls on the truck?"

"If I can."

"And if you can't?"

"I owe a man and a woman a favour. That favour is Cassy. She is my priority."

"And then what?"

"Excuse me?"

"You murder my husband. You save the girl. You ride off into the sunset. Then what?"

He searched for his heart pills.

She reached into her pocket and handed them to him.

He snatched them and swallowed two.

"I shouldn't have fucked you," Sullivan decided.

"Why?"

"Because of this."

"This has nothing to do with us fucking."

"What is it to do with?"

"You and your stupid idea that you have to be some wandering nomad."

He punched the wall.

Enough!

He moved his face within inches of hers.

She didn't blink or falter.

"People I love die. My wife. My daughter, who didn't die, but is pretty much dead to me. Connor. Elsie. I bring bad luck to everyone, and I don't want to bother with that shit. I just want to see out my final days, somewhere away from people who moan at me about who I am. Alone. Completely, utterly alone."

He held his face there, sneering, almost growling.

She did not break. Not one bit.

She ran a gentle, smooth palm down his bristly cheek, and whispered, "I'm going out for some cigarettes and to get you some more clothes. Get some sleep."

241

"Get me a knife too. A sharp one."

She stepped toward the door and paused. Looked back. Smiled at him.

"People I love die too, you know," she said, and left.

Sullivan watched the door for a while, thinking very little. Once he realised he hadn't moved in a while, he climbed into bed and pulled the duvet over himself. He didn't expect to get much sleep, but he'd try.

For a moment, he wished she was there next to him.

THE TYRRHENUM SEA

CHAPTER FORTY-NINE

HER EYES OPENED.

She was expecting to see the sun. Sky. Her room. Something.

All Cassy saw was darkness.

She was cold. Still so cold.

The truck seemed to have stopped, and there were voices outside of it. They were deep and menacing.

However asleep she'd somehow found herself a moment ago, she was now awake and alert. Still trapped. No idea where she was going, but knowing it was nowhere good.

She wanted to cry, but who would listen?

She wanted to ask for help, but who would care?

There were so many girls in such a small space, but they were all still alone.

Completely alone.

"Hey," came a voice.

Cassy assumed it was a brush of wind from outside, or a shuffle of clothes or a grunt in someone's sleep.

But it spoke again.

"Hey," it said.

She turned to her right.

In the darkness she could make out a faint line. Someone crouched on the floor like her. Shivering.

"What's your name?" the voice asked. It was a whisper, so Cassy couldn't tell much about it, but she could tell it was a young voice. But not that young. Someone her age, or possibly a little older.

"Cassy," she said.

"Where are you from?" the girl asked.

"Frome."

"Where's that?"

"I – I don't know."

She was sure she knew, but for whatever reason, she couldn't form the words.

Wherever she was from, she wasn't there now.

Grandad. Grandma. They were dead.

She bowed her head and allowed herself a few tears, careful to keep them silent.

The girl she had been speaking to moved beside Cassy. She felt arms wrap around her. She didn't fight it. In fact, she leant her head on the girl's shoulder.

It was bony. The girl's hair fell in her face. It smelt musky. Like smoke. The girl's body smelt like dry sweat. Cassy didn't care. She was terrified, and she needed a friend.

"My name is Madeline," the girl said.

She could hear her voice now. It wasn't an English accent. It was foreign. French, maybe?

She didn't ask where from. It didn't matter.

"Do you know where we're going?" Madeline asked.

Cassy shrugged, then, realising she couldn't be seen, answered, "No."

The awareness that she had no idea where she was going dawned on her again, as if her thoughts were just one big cycle:

tiredness, sadness for Grandad and Grandma's death, terror for not knowing where she was, and repeat.

"Neither do I," Madeline said.

"Do you think they will kill all of us?" Cassy asked.

"No."

"Why?"

"Because they would have done it by now. I heard one man saying they need to deliver us somewhere."

"Where?"

"I don't know."

Cassy shook her head. Tightened her eyes.

How had she ended up here? Where was here? And if they weren't going to kill her, what were they going to do to her?

"Let's make a deal, Cassy. Wherever they take us, we stick together. Yeah? Whatever, we stick together."

Cassy nodded.

"Okay," she said.

And for a moment, it comforted her.

That was, until the cycle began once again with tiredness, sadness, then terror.

ODESSA, UKRAINE

CHAPTER FIFTY

Sullivan and Charlene discarded the rental car in the town centre and walked to the nearest phone shop, where Charlene bought two iPhones. She sat on a bench while she set them up and Sullivan found them some food. Once Charlene had finished, they made their way to the dock.

There were dozens of ships pulling in to various ports.

How were they meant to tell which one Cassy was on? And, even if they did, how would they find the right truck?

"Shit," he said.

"Don't worry," Charlene said. "It's that one there."

She pointed at a ship arriving a few ports over.

"You sure?"

"I think I know my husband's ship."

She withdrew one of the iPhones and hit the screen a few times. Once she had finished, she took out another iPhone and did the same.

"What are you–"

"Hang on."

His fists clenched.

"Right," she declared, handing him one of the phones.

"What's this?"

"See this circle?" She pointed to a circle on a map displayed on the screen of this device. "That's me."

"How is that you?"

She waved her iPhone.

"How'd you do that?" he asked.

"It's an app called Find My iPhone. The two devices are connected. You can watch where my iPhone goes."

"Seriously?"

"Yes. Why do you seem so astonished? Don't you have a phone?"

"No."

Sullivan hadn't particularly needed a phone. He was aware enough to know they were all the rage nowadays, but he had no use for one. He wasn't on social media. He had no one to call and he did not want to leave any form of digital trace. He'd only ever used a phone to receive contracts and use the maps app, that was all.

He stared at the screen. At the little dot blinking at him.

Was this really possible?

Tracking a device like this was something expertly trained Falcons used to do covertly. It was something secret organisations did with high-tech devices. Now you could just download an app and do it yourself?

He realised just how out of touch he was.

"I'm going onto the boat," she said. "I'll tell Hugo I came to surprise him, that I did it because I want to work at this marriage. Play the doting wife."

"How will I know when you've found him?"

"The dot will be still. I'll have stopped moving. I'll keep Hugo between me and the door."

"What are you going to do to distract him?"

She shrugged. "Whatever I have to."

"And what about the customs officials?"

"They'll let Hugo's wife on. If not, I have enough money to bribe them. I assume you do too?"

"I know how to sneak aboard a ship without getting caught."

"You are a man of many talents."

A moment of harmonious silence fell between them.

"I guess I'll be seeing you," she said.

"I guess so."

She turned to walk away. Stopped. Turned back, a few steps between them, and held Sullivan's gaze.

"You know," she said, "after all this is over, I'm going to have to be on the run too. People will be after me. I'll have to disappear."

"Oh yeah?"

"It would be nice to have someone to disappear with."

Sullivan bowed his head. Sighed. This again?

"Do you really not think about having a future?" she asked.

"I've known you for a few days."

"A few days is enough."

"Charlene, I..."

He exhaled.

How was he supposed to get this through to her?

"I'm not your way out," he said.

She smiled. Stepped forward. Kissed him on the cheek.

"People might see us," Sullivan said.

"Do you always do the sensible thing?"

"Rarely. But I'm trying."

She stepped away. Tucked her phone into her inside jacket pocket, turned, and walked to the ship to find her husband.

CHAPTER FIFTY-ONE

A STING OF FEAR CLUTCHED CHARLENE'S STOMACH AS SHE approached the boat. Nerves clung to her chest. She felt queasy. Nauseous.

What was she doing?

She'd never done anything like this before. She'd always stuck to her wifely roles. Brought up the children. Made tea. Went to book club. Did the parent's evenings. Entertained Hugo's friends by bringing them beers and food. Rubbed his shoulders as he watched television.

She did everything the delicate wife of a hardened criminal was meant to do.

But she wasn't delicate.

Not anymore.

Maybe she was when she met him. Back when she was young. Weak. Vulnerable. Full of hope that some man would take her off her feet and show her a life where she'd never have to worry.

And maybe she'd had that, once.

But then he killed my son.

The thought overpowered her trepidation, and she clung onto it for strength as she boarded the ship.

Before Nathaniel was murdered, she was that dainty woman. Fragile. Weak. She'd envied strong women. Always wished she could be one.

Now she was going to show strong women how it was done.

She was no longer withdrawn. She was fierce.

No longer submissive. She was dominant.

No longer a pushover. She was determined.

She made it onto the vehicle deck. Passed the trucks. Walked up the stairs, her heels echoing on metal steps as she made her way to the top deck.

The view of Odessa was incredible. A beautiful city. There were beaches. Grand architecture. Clean water leading to the Black Sea. A perfect disguise for what the city hid.

She supposed that, like her, cities often hid their darkness beneath their beauty.

She and Sullivan could disappear here. To begin with, anyway. Then they could drive to Romania and go from there. He would fight it, but he didn't want to be alone any more than she did. She knew it.

She snapped her mind back into focus. Searched the deck for Hugo.

There he was. Standing by the rail, surrounded by thugs. Men in suits with meaty heads and sunglasses, like they were trying to imitate a cliché from a movie.

She took a deep breath, held it, and willed herself to put on the best performance possible.

She approached him.Quelled the nerves. Put on a smile.

"Hey, honey," she said, her voice low and smooth, just as she knew would excite him.

Well, it used to excite him. She imagined he was bored with her now. Her showing up would probably disappoint him inside, as he most likely had a mistress or two waiting for him here.

He turned around.

"Charlene?" he said. "What are you doing here?"

She didn't answer him. She just stepped toward him, put her arms on his side and leant in, kissing him in front of all his goons. Slipped her tongue into his mouth. Gently stroked it against his. Showing off that he got to kiss this bombshell of a woman and they didn't.

He grew hard against her waist.

"I thought I would surprise you."

"How did you get here?"

"I drove. Thought you might like a surprise."

Hugo looked to be toying with appreciation, but she could tell he was also angry.

"Can we go somewhere private?" she asked. "Have you got five minutes?"

She winked. Licked her lips. Subtly ran her hand across his crotch.

"Sure," he said, nodding vacantly. "We have five minutes."

He looked to his men.

"If I'm not back in ten minutes, unload without me."

"Take me to your room," she whispered into his ear, knowing her hot breath would make him tingle.

"Sure," he said. He walked, cautiously, and she followed. He was evidently thrown. Not expecting this.

She took his hand and allowed him to lead her.

CHAPTER FIFTY-TWO

BACK AT IT AGAIN.

Assassin-mode, like the old days.

Except, not as astute.

Sullivan felt sluggish. Less observant. Ill-prepared.

He needed to get over that.

He sneaked aboard the vehicle deck.

There were a lot of trucks, and a lot of men with their guns partially concealed, standing up and down the deck. Most of these trucks would be full of stolen goods or drugs, which would probably be of equal value to Hugo as the girls. He had no idea which truck Cassy was in, and trying to find her would be useless; he would not be able to search every truck and kill every man. There were at least thirty trucks, and even more armed men. The first lesson he'd ever been taught was not to enter a fight he couldn't win. Five or six of these men, possibly even a few more, and he would be prepared to take them out. But this many? And all of them armed? He didn't stand a chance.

He needed Hugo for either information, or for leverage.

The hardest part would be leaving this vehicle deck,

knowing one of these trucks had Cassy on. But he was outnumbered. He had to be sensible. Think with his rational mind, not his wayward melancholy.

He tucked the iPhone into the back of his trousers and held onto the knife Charlene had acquired for him whilst he slept in the motel.

The door to the stairs was halfway along the deck. He couldn't get there by just staying low and using the cars as cover. They were patrolling. Moving. If one of them discovered him, the rest would turn and shoot.

He would go under the trucks.

He moved onto his belly, keeping the knife in his hand just in case. He crawled forward, picking up debris on the ground and staining his shirt.

Not ideal. But didn't matter. He'd buy new clothes.

He just hated ruining a good suit.

He made his way underneath the first truck. Shimmied forward, pushing his feet and dragging with his hands. Flexing his fingers on the hand of the knife, just in case he needed to use it.

He reached the edge of the first truck.

Looked out.

A man walked past, talking idly with another.

"We ready to go?"

"Just waiting."

"What for?"

"Hugo's go ahead."

"We're all set. What's he waiting for?"

"You want to take it up with Hugo?"

"...I'll wait."

Keeping his footsteps light and silent, Sullivan moved from the bottom of one truck to the other.

He'd passed about ten or eleven trucks when the door to the stairs came into view.

A man guarded it.

Sullivan waited for the man to move, but he didn't. The man stayed there, stationary, staring absently at nothing.

Sullivan searched for something on the ground. A stone, or rock, or debris, or something.

He found a stone. Crawled along the underside of the truck.

Threw the stone as far into the opposite direction.

The man quickly turned to look, and a few of the men walked away from Sullivan to see what it was.

This was his chance.

He ran out from beneath the truck.

The man saw him and turned to fire his gun. Sullivan knocked the gun away and swung the knife across the man's throat.

He placed a foot behind the man's ankle and pushed him to the floor. He crouched beside him, keeping a hand over the man's mouth as he fought for breath. Blood squirted all over his sleeve, but the man was dying silently, and that's what mattered.

Sullivan waited to see if anyone had heard or seen him, but no one reacted. No one said anything.

He waited a little longer for the man to die, then took away his hand. The sleeve of his shirt was completely red. He wiped it on the man's face to ensure it didn't drip; he did not want to leave a trail. He dragged the body beneath the nearest vehicle, moved to the stairs, opened the door, and sneaked in.

He strode up a few steps and stopped. Took out the iPhone. The dot no longer moved. It was a little further along the boat.

He ran up the stairs, keeping his knife ready.

CHAPTER FIFTY-THREE

CHARLENE CLOSED THE DOOR BEHIND HER AND MADE HER way toward the bed.

Hugo stood between her and the door.

She removed her jacket. Removed her top. Removed her skirt. Stood, wearing nothing but red-laced underwear and high heels.

Hugo did not move toward her. Nor did he retreat. He just watched her, standing by the door, matching her knowing grin.

"Well?" she prompted. "Are you not going to come and take what's yours?"

"What's mine?" he repeated, like it was a joke she wasn't in on.

"Yes. What is yours."

She crawled onto the bed and remained on all fours. Looked up at him with a sexy pout that would normally make men go crazy.

"Well?" she added.

He chuckled.

"You really are trying, aren't you?"

"What do you mean? Of course I'm trying. I want us to work."

"It just strikes me as odd."

She turned around so he could see her buttocks poking out from either side of her thong.

"Nothing odd about it," she said, keeping her voice low, sultry, sexy.

"Well, you certainly do look nice," he said.

"Nice?"

She was a little offended, but she persevered, kept playing her part.

She moved to her knees. Opened her mouth, enticing him to come closer and enter her in whichever way he saw fit.

He did not come closer. He did not enter her. But he did take off his jacket and dump it on the chair.

"That's a good start," she said. "Now how about the rest?"

He undid his cuffs. Rolled up his sleeves.

"Honey?" she said.

Why wasn't he coming closer? Why wasn't he taking her?

She slumped down, a little thrown. She reminded herself to be sexy. To be seductive. She moved to all fours again, crawling toward him across the bed.

"I'm waiting," she said.

"Indeed, you are, my dear. Indeed, you are."

She frowned. What was going on?

"And this performance," he continued. "I assume this is all just for me?"

"It's all for you."

"Ah, brilliant. And can I just ask one question, my dearest?"

"By all means."

"Okay."

He put his hands in his pockets. Raised his eyebrows. Sighed.

"Do you think I'm a fucking idiot?"

She had no answer. She did not understand. Where had this come from?

"I would actually like you to answer that question."

"Baby, I–"

"Don't *baby* me."

"I don't understand."

"Evidently."

"I just wanted to surprise you."

"Surprise me? Weeks of not touching me, of wallowing over pictures of Nathaniel, of being the most miserable bitch you can — and now you *surprise* me?"

"I was just sad, but it's okay now, I understand that you had to–"

Hugo thumped the wall. Cracks formed in the weak plaster.

"The truth," he demanded.

"What truth, baby?"

"Stop calling me baby."

"But I always call you–"

He thumped the wall again. Harder. This time her body convulsed in shock.

Her arms trembled. She suddenly felt very naked.

Is this how I will die? In my underwear, on a boat that's trafficking girls?

She imagined her body being found like this. Barely dressed. A corpse without dignity. Then she hated herself for being so concerned with what she would be wearing when her body was discovered.

"Honey, I just–" she said, stopping as she saw Hugo take a gun from his belt. "What are you doing?"

Hugo lay the gun on a cupboard.

"I was going to use this," he said. "But I think it's too quick a death. Far more than a lying whore is worth."

"I'm not lying."

He chuckled. She hated that chuckle. That chuckle scared her more than any wall punch or gun.

"I knew it would come to this," he said. "Somehow, I knew."

"I don't understand…"

He crawled onto the bed. Kneeling before her. His face inches from hers.

"You must think I'm the world's biggest fool for trusting you this long."

"Honey…"

"I always knew you'd betray me. I'm just glad I'm the one who gets to give you your comeuppance."

She went to respond, but his hands around her throat stopped her.

His thumbs pressed against her windpipe.

She struggled for breath that didn't come.

He forced her onto her back, the softness of the bed contrasting with the deadly image of her husband above her.

Where was Sullivan? Why wasn't he here?

She tried to fight him off, battered his arms with hers, punched with all she had. It did nothing. He was too strong.

She tried to say something. Words almost formed, and he grinned at her desperation to speak.

She persisted, her mouth opening and closing like a fish.

He gave into temptation. He loosened her throat for a moment and looked at her with a face full of mocking.

"What?" he said. "Tell me, please, what are your dying words?"

She glared at him more intently than she had ever glared before. She spoke her final words slowly, enunciating every syllable with as much spite as she was able, knowing nothing would stop him killing her now, so she may as well say what she wanted.

"Jay Sullivan was a far better fuck than *you*."

His face contorted.

Now that had hurt.

He pushing his thumbs harder against her windpipe, pressing and pressing until she stopped struggling.

CHAPTER FIFTY-FOUR

RUMBLES FROM THE VEHICLE DECK BELOW CONFIRMED TO Sullivan what he dreaded.

The trucks were turning on their engines. Soon, they would leave the ship.

He needed to get to Charlene quickly, do whatever he needed with Hugo, and get below.

Years ago, this would have been a plan of stealth. Now it was skilful improvisation at best.

He stopped creeping and began running.

He checked the iPhone. The dot was close. Just down this corridor.

As he turned the corner, he saw the room. Two men stood outside it. Guns held across their chests. Dead faced, and dead eyed.

Here we go...

Sullivan ditched the subtlety and sprinted, his knife ready.

The men saw him. They turned and aimed their guns.

Before either of their fingers could press their trigger, Sullivan had slid to his knees and sliced his knife upwards through the first man's groin.

He stood, sticking his knife through the cheek of the second man.

Turning back to the first man, he sliced the knife across his throat, then returned to the other and punched the gun out of his hand. He ducked a strike and swung the knife into the underside of his chin.

The knife stuck through his mouth, but did not reach the brain. He was still alive. Still, it meant Sullivan's opponent did not fight back, what with him having to compete with the blood gargling out of his mouth.

Sullivan considered taking the gun and shooting him, but he didn't want to make that much noise. Hugo was in that room. He did not want to alarm him with gun sounds. Hopefully, Charlene was occupying him enough that he wouldn't notice the sounds of a scuffle. So, instead, he finished the man off with the simple slice of his throat.

Rumblings of vehicles driving below grew louder. They were all leaving. He hadn't much time.

Sullivan turned to the door. Readied his knife. Kicked it open and burst in.

He went to attack, but there was nothing to attack.

Charlene lay on the bed.

He was confused. Why was she laying on the bed? Why was she–

Her chest was still. Was she breathing?

He ran to her side.

Her eyes stared wide and absently at the ceiling. Her body laid out.

She had been suffocated.

He bowed his head. Stupid woman.

This was what happened when you trusted Jay Sullivan.

"Drop the weapon," came a voice from behind him, and he turned.

Hugo sat on a chair in the room's corner, a gun pointed at Sullivan's temple.

CHAPTER FIFTY-FIVE

Cassy had unknowingly found her hand in Madeline's.

They still shook. Still squirmed with fear. Still shuddered with terror. But they did it together.

Clutching each other, refusing to let go.

The voices outside the truck grew louder. Doors opened and closed in the vehicle's cab.

A rumble of ignition gently shook the truck.

"What's happening?" Cassy whispered.

Some other girls started waking up. It was still so dark, and their eyes could only adjust so much; she could see the outline of other girls huddled up, trembling, as alone and scared as each other.

"I'm not sure," Madeline whispered back.

A jolt and the vehicle moved. Slowly at first. They fell on top of each other as the truck flung around a big corner, and then it picked up speed.

"Where is it taking us?"

"I don't know."

Faint voices came from the cab. Laughing and joking. Male.

A language she didn't understand. An accent she didn't recognise.

"That's..." Madeline listened. "Polish. Or Ukrainian. Russian. Something Eastern European."

Madeline was saying names of places Cassy didn't know. Yet, even though she didn't know of these places, she still knew she was far from home.

"Will you stay with me?" she asked.

Madeline gripped Cassy's hand harder.

The truck came to a stop.

More voices came from outside the truck. Cassy didn't understand the few words that made it through, but they sounded inquisitive, like they were asking questions.

Could they be here to help them? Could this person, or these people, be asking where this truck is going?

What if they asked to see inside? Discovered them? Would they be freed?

She felt hope. Her heart raced. Adrenaline made her legs shake harder.

"What is it?" Madeline asked, still keeping her voice hushed.

"That voice — he's not one of them. I'm sure of it."

Madeline strained to hear.

"Should we shout or something?" Madeline asked.

Cassy thought about shouting, then remembered how the girl had died for making noise. "If it's not someone come to help and they hear us shouting, and then they..."

She trailed off as the voice left and the truck began moving once again.

Hope diminished. Grave desperation returned. A sickness that Cassy couldn't fight.

"I don't think they were here to save us," Madeline said.

Cassy didn't respond. She was still hoping they hadn't

moved. That someone was there. That, at any moment, the truck would open and they would be freed.

It didn't take long until she resettled into the sense of foreboding she had become accustomed to.

CHAPTER FIFTY-SIX

THIS WASN'T THE FIRST TIME SULLIVAN HAD A GUN POINTED at him.

And he had full confidence it wouldn't be the last.

Which made him wonder; why hadn't Hugo pulled the trigger already?

Hugo would know who his opponent was. Whether Sullivan still had the skills he once had was debatable, but his reputation still made him out to be a formidable opponent.

He looked to Charlene. Laying still. Thumb prints marked in red on her throat.

Hugo hadn't shot his wife; he'd suffocated her. This was not a professional death.

This was a vindictive death.

Hugo had chosen a far slower, painful method on purpose. He'd wanted Charlene to suffer. He'd wanted to feel the hope and the life escape her.

Foolish Charlene. You should have just taken your kids and ran.

"Don't look at her," Hugo instructed.

Ah. Now that was why he wasn't dead yet.

Hugo needed to know.

If Hugo had chosen such a long, drawn-out death rather than a quick, professional kill, then that made this a kill of passion, not necessity.

Passion was fuelled by betrayal.

Sullivan did not think the passion with which Hugo had murdered his wife came from a feeling of love; it was pride. It dented his ego that another man had touched his wife, and he wanted to know how far her betrayal had gone. It was his wife; he *had* to know.

Sullivan gazed upon her empty eyes. Deliberately, knowing it would incense Hugo.

"I said stop it."

He didn't stop it.

"Stop it!"

Hugo flipped the nearby bedside table. Sullivan noticed a dent in the plaster behind him the size of a fist.

Sullivan looked at Hugo, patiently and expectantly. Watching his opponent. Trying to figure out how to play this.

"Get on your knees."

Sullivan did as he was told, holding his hands in the air, listening to the sounds of the vehicles below leaving.

He was losing Cassy. It wouldn't be long until the truck she was on disappeared into the underbelly of Ukraine.

He stared at Charlene, infuriating Hugo, hoping to make him reckless.

"I know what you're doing," Hugo stated.

Sullivan smiled. He traced his eyes down Charlene's body. So still, so beautiful. Such a waste.

"Tell me," Hugo said, aiming his gun. "Did you fuck her?"

Sullivan looked at Hugo. He didn't speak.

"Answer the question," Hugo insisted.

Sullivan was tempted to confirm, just to see the look on Hugo's face.

I don't think I fucked her so much as she fucked me.

The quip was poised on the edge of his lips, but he kept it inside.

If he gave an answer, that would be it. The end. Hugo would discover the extent of his wife's betrayal, and he would have no reason to wait any longer in pulling the trigger.

"You think this is funny?" Hugo asked. "Amusing? Hilarious? Is that why you are keeping silent?"

Sullivan smirked. "Keeping silent about what?"

"Stop it! Stop it, stop it, stop it! Stop acting like she did nothing. You think I don't know my wife? You think you're the first idiot she came onto? I bet she'd planned to run away with you, hadn't she? *Hadn't she?*"

Sullivan didn't answer. He was astonished to finally see what it looked like when Hugo actually lost control. He felt proud that he was the one who'd caused it.

Hugo's lip sneered. His face was an ugly grimace, a mixture of anger and futility.

Sullivan could only hold on without answering for so long. Soon, Hugo would just assume.

He looked to the bed. Moving just his eyes, not his face. There was a space under the bed.

How thick was that mattress?

Not thick enough to stop bullets.

But, if he moved himself under the bed and stayed directly beneath the body, her corpse would block any bullets. She could protect him in death.

He studied her position, looking at how she lay. Her head lolling to the right. Her arm splayed out. Her legs to the side.

"Answer me. Did you, or did you not, fuck my wife?"

Sullivan finished studying the corpse.

The beautiful corpse.

The goddamn tragedy of a corpse.

"Yes," he said, grinning, then rolled beneath the bed, assuming the position of the body.

CHAPTER FIFTY-SEVEN

HUGO LAUNCHED HIMSELF ONTO THE BED AND UNLOADED the gun, firing his rage into the mattress, tufts of feather and wayward springs responding.

He fired all over. Through Charlene's body, around Charlene's body, everywhere he was able, until he found himself pulling the trigger and the click of an empty clip responding.

The instant that click sounded, the bed lifted and Hugo fell to his back, flailing beneath the upturned mattress.

If his rage hadn't been immense before, it was immense now. He'd never felt this amount of anger before. Not even at Nathaniel. For his wife to not only betray him, but to fuck the enemy...

With a roar, Hugo threw off the mattress.

The door was open. The cabin was empty.

The bodies of his security guards lay on the floor.

"Fucking charlatans," he muttered, charging out of the room.

Sullivan disappeared down the end of the corridor. Hugo took a gun from his dead guards and fired, narrowly missing Sullivan's head as he turned the corner.

Hugo sprinted.

Sullivan turned another corner, and a few more of Hugo's bullets hit the wall.

Hugo passed a few of his men.

"Get him!"

They radioed it in and followed Hugo to the stairs. Within seconds, he had a full entourage behind him of big, burly men with even bigger guns.

They pounded up the steps onto the deck. There Sullivan was, staring as the coast of Odessa moved further away.

That's when Sullivan appeared to realise they were leaving Ukraine. All the trucks had left the ship, and they were returning to sea, ready to return home.

Hugo enjoyed the look on Sullivan's face as he saw that he'd lost, and that he was stuck on this ship with nowhere to go. Any chance of finding the girl disappeared. He was normally so cocky, now he looked deeply despondent.

Sullivan leapt from the top deck to the lower deck, falling on his arm as he did. He ignored any pain, got up, and ran.

"Get him," Hugo instructed, and his men pursued, each of them leaping from the top deck to the bottom deck, just as Sullivan had done.

As he watched his men approach the target, Hugo took aim.

Sullivan was running erratically. Sprinting back and forth in a chaotic line. Most would look at this and think he was acting crazily. Hugo knew this was to evade any potential shots.

But Sullivan was running to the end of the boat. He had nowhere else to go.

Hugo smiled as his men approached Sullivan.

Sullivan looked at the sea below. At the clear ocean that began their return journey.

The trucks had already gone.

The ship was at sea.

Hugo was sure this was it, was positive that they had him. He could not have expected Sullivan to be so foolish to do what he did next.

Sullivan locked eyes with Hugo, presented his middle finger, and let himself fall from the boat with a glorious splash.

Hugo's men looked at him for instructions.

"What are you looking at me for? Shoot him!"

They obediently fired a stream of bullets into the water where Sullivan had just fallen.

CHAPTER FIFTY-EIGHT

CHARLES HAD STUMBLED OFF THE BOAT AND INTO UKRAINE as a free man. He looked over his shoulder, back at the ship. Already returning to the ocean.

He was free, but it was tainted.

He had toyed with his conscience for the whole journey. He'd made a poor attempt at helping the girl, and it wasn't good enough.

But what was he supposed to do? Confront dozens of armed men?

He'd never been in a fight in his life.

He'd been beaten up, but not in a fight. A fight suggests that it is two-sided. He had never retaliated to anything.

Even when his wife and he argued, and she was in the wrong, he would apologise.

When he was convicted for his offence, he admitted it and requested leniency.

He had done so much wrong. He wasn't capable of doing anything right.

As he finally forced his eyes away from the ship, his gaze

fell on the line of trucks that had departed the boat and were now driving into the country.

Wasn't Hugo worried Charles would say something? Wouldn't he want Charles dead?

Charles snorted.

Charles wasn't a threat. Hugo murdered his wife, and Charles still went crawling back. Hugo probably hadn't even given Charles a second thought. Besides, Hugo may be a criminal, but he was also a man of his word. When Charles had delivered the girl and that man, he knew Hugo would follow through.

He watched the stream of trucks driving casually, under the speed limit, dispersing into the city. A city of culture and beauty that did not know what evil had just entered it.

He looked to the beach next to the docks. Families laughed, couples sunbathed. Some boy played ball with his dad. A few girls ran into the sea.

How could none of them have any idea?

Then he saw it. The truck. Despite its similarity to the others, there was something about the way the mud marked its rear that sparked a sense of familiarity.

He thought of what the truck contained.

Cassy. Other girls. Taken from their homes. Vulnerable girls people wouldn't ask about. Girls that no one would miss.

Charles did the only thing he could. He read the licence plate aloud, and kept repeating it until he had the letters and numbers memorised.

It wasn't a Ukrainian licence plate. It was a British one. That would make it stand out a little.

And now what? Now he had that licence plate, what would he do with it?

What if he went to the police? The authorities would know what to do.

He quickly realised what a bad idea that would be. Chances

were, the people in power had already been handsomely paid or severely threatened for their silence. If some idiot came along babbling his head off about some licence plate, they would alert Hugo.

Hugo, ever a man of his word, was also a man who demanded loyalty. If Hugo murdered Charles' wife over a little debt, then what would Hugo do with a rat?

Then again, say Hugo killed Charles over it... would Charles not deserve it?

This was a chance to make amends. A moment where he could at least attempt to do the right thing.

He told his legs to move. To take him into the city centre. To use a map to take him to the police station. To go there and ask to speak to someone in private, someone who spoke English. He'd open his mouth and out would come the inevitable endless chatter, going on and on about everything that had happened.

But his legs hadn't moved.

And his mouth was closed.

Who was he kidding? He was a cowardly piece of shit. He would not do the right thing. He would do whatever it took to survive.

He had the licence plate, but it didn't matter.

He put his head down. Stepped onto the road. He was so engrossed in his thoughts; he didn't notice the speeding car coming.

It drove into him and sent him hurtling over its windshield.

Charles lay in a pool of blood on the road.

The car sped off.

People around him stood in shock. Someone called an ambulance.

CHAPTER FIFTY-NINE

Bullets streamed through the water, and Sullivan had no choice but to go deeper and deeper.

He didn't get a good look at what type of weapons they were, but he knew he needed to sink at least ten feet below surface until he felt confident the bullets couldn't be fatal.

The direction of bullets under water was unpredictable, and their trajectory could change, so trying to dodge any was not an option. The speed of bullets slows in water, but this can depend upon the weapon. A .50 calibre can disintegrate at three feet. Slower velocity bullets, such as a pistol, would take up to eight feet. A shotgun might take longer.

The lower he sank, the more likely he'd avoid being hit.

Only problem was, the lower he sank, the further away he was from oxygen.

He had no choice.

He swam. Forced himself downwards, watching lines appearing around him.

Once he was deep enough, he focussed on swimming forward. The ship was moving away from him, and he figured it wouldn't be long until they couldn't see where he was anymore.

But the bullets still came. They were determined, he'd give them that.

His heart was raging again. The strain he was putting on it needed to be quelled with pills, but he couldn't stop to take any. He hadn't time.

A healthy person might last two minutes underwater without oxygen. Sullivan, unfortunately, was not a healthy person. A body destroyed by alcohol and neglect, and a difficult heart problem, meant he would probably not have so long.

He was already getting dizzy.

Adrenaline was fuelling him, but he was using a lot of energy. His arms and legs thrashed him forward. He would need oxygen soon.

If he could just get closer to shore...

The boat would need to turn around to follow him. It would take a boat that size too long. He could beat it if he just put more distance between them.

He just had to get far enough away that their bullets wouldn't hit him.

But the boat was still there, drifting away, but so slowly. The bullets were parading around him at such a high frequency.

He needed oxygen. He had no choice.

He pushed himself upwards. Forced his arms to thrash and his legs to kick.

His face rose above the surface.

He took in a big gulp of air.

Took more. Again and again. Taking in as much oxygen as his lungs would take.

He saw Hugo at the edge of the ship.

"There he is!"

Guns aimed at him, and more bullets came.

He plunged himself back down.

He swam at an angle, moving closer to the shore whilst sinking deeper.

His body felt so heavy. His arms ached. He'd done too much running, too much fighting.

What would happen if he just let go? Let himself be shot? Let himself drown?

The truck was gone. Disappeared into the city, amongst many others. He had no way of finding it. No chance of saving Cassy.

No. I have to keep trying.

The instinct to fight was strong. It was the instinct he'd had his whole life. That's why it was so hard to accept that he had lost the fight.

She was gone.

They outnumbered him.

And the shore was too far away.

Just as the temptation to give in and let this pathetic little life of his go, a searing pain hit his calf.

He turned and looked.

Blood floated from his leg.

There was no bullet in him; it must have just scraped his skin. But it was enough for him to lose blood, and he was losing it quickly.

Within seconds, blood was all he could see.

Perhaps they'd think he was dead and give up.

No, these people were professionals. Sullivan would never confirm a hit without a target, and neither would they. They would need to see his body. He just had to stay conscious long enough to make it to shore, then go from there.

He swam, ignoring the pain growing in his calf, the pain in his chest, and the hammering in his head.

CHAPTER SIXTY

"Turn the ship around!" Hugo demanded.

"But boss, we got him, look at the blood–"

"He might just be wounded for all we know. I want a body. Do it!"

"We'd have to inform the coast guard and the shipyard that we need somewhere to dock."

Hugo grabbed the man by the throat.

"Do I look like I give a fuck about the sodding coast guard? Tell them to make way for us, and tell them to turn the ship. *Now.*"

As his lackey scuttled off to do his bidding, Hugo charged up the deck of the boat, peering into the water below. Blood floated upwards. A lot of it. Maybe sharks would smell it and do his bidding for him. Maybe Sullivan's heavy corpse was sinking further down.

But he wasn't. Beyond the mass of blood below was a trail of blood directed toward shore. Beyond that, Hugo could not see anything. The blood trail led too far away

It would be pointless to shoot. They should conserve their

bullets until the ship had finished turning. It began its large rotation, its nose turning to the left.

Hugo stayed at the railings, watching the trail of red to ensure they did not lose him, but it was no good. The ship was taking too long. The trail of blood was growing thinner.

"Hurry it up!" Hugo shouted, knowing that there would be nothing they could do to hurry it up. Any quicker and the boat would capsize.

His hands gripped the railings, and the cold metal hurt his palm.

This man tried to mess with Hugo's business.

This man escaped Phillipe twice.

And, most painstaking of all, this man had fucked his wife.

Hugo wanted to see him die. Wanted to hold the bastard's corpse. Wanted to snarl at his empty, dead face.

He knew anger was clouding his judgement. He knew all eyes were on him, all his men, all the crew, everyone — because they had never seen him lose his calm before.

For his whole life, whatever the situation, he had exuded confidence and composure. Even when killing his son, he only spoke when he needed to.

Almost fifty years, and that facade was broken by one pitiable ex-assassin and his own stupid wife.

He had lost more than his wife. He had lost his power. His ruthless nature.

He had allowed everyone to see his fury.

The ship's rotation continued. It was taking too fucking long.

His hands were gripping harder. His nails grating the metal. The sweat of his palms loosening his grip.

He roared. Screamed. Let out a cry of anguish.

He would not let this bastard escape.

He would not.

He would see to Sullivan's capture himself, witness his

torture and his death, his impeccable death, his long, drawn-out death. He would grind Sullivan's bones and stretch his muscles and remove his teeth and fry his dick and break his jaw. He would find anyone Sullivan may still care about and do the same, torture them as Sullivan cried and begged for mercy.

No one dared speak to him.

No one wanted to face this wrath.

The boat finally finished turning and headed back to dock.

CHAPTER SIXTY-ONE

IT WAS TOO MUCH.

His arms wouldn't carry him any further.

His muscles were empty yet heavy. His body was done. He couldn't power through even if he wanted to.

The shore was so close. Just a few more minutes and he'd make it, Sullivan knew it.

But it was too far.

Even oxygen wouldn't save him now.

His body lacked blood. He'd lost too much. The trail behind him was long.

He'd lost. It was time to accept it.

He would not go down fighting. He would not go down in surrender.

He stopped swimming. Just floated. He couldn't feel his body anymore. His arms wouldn't even steady him.

The sun above was harsh, and it blurred his vision.

They would use Cassy as an underage whore. She would have a fate she could no longer escape.

Sullivan was going to die. He knew it.

He wondered if Talia would find out.

Probably. Hugo would want to declare his victory to the world. There would be nothing to stop him.

Sullivan deserved it.

He did.

He'd hoped for redemption, but instead, he'd received his penance.

No one else would die because of him.

He closed his eyes.

He didn't fight it any longer.

He allowed the waves to carry him back and forth, to move a body absent of fight.

His mind faded and he saw Talia's smile. It was his wife's smile. But it wasn't real.

He would never see that smile again.

He lost consciousness.

He had lost.

OUTSIDE OF LVIV, UKRAINE

CHAPTER SIXTY-TWO

THE RUMBLE OF THE TRUCK'S ENGINE GREW QUIETER, AND the truck stopped.

The engine died.

Silence followed.

The sobbing of the other girls had stopped. It was as if they were all on edge, knowing they were about to find out what horrors were waiting for them.

Cassy dreaded what would appear when they dragged her off that truck. She wondered whether they would let her and Madeline stay together.

When the truck doors opened, the blinding sunshine was the first thing to hit her.

Someone said something in a language she didn't know. She squinted, trying to see who it was. Once her eyes had adjusted, she saw a large, burly man. Lots of tattoos on his neck and arms. His head was like a boulder, hairless and hard. His face was grim. He held a gun across his chest with pride.

"Zabryasya," he said in a low, growling voice.

No one moved.

"Get out!" he said, in a thick accent, and a few of the girls cautiously crawled forward, but none of them attempted to leave the truck.

It was strange; they had wanted so desperately to escape this truck, and now they had the opportunity to leave it, no one wanted to take it.

Finally, the man turned to his right and waved to a few people.

"Davayte vyvedemon yikh."

More men, almost identical, came into the light. Skinhead. Muscular. Tattoos. Armed.

They dragged the girls out, one by one.

Being the girls furthest into the truck, all Cassy and Madeline could do was watch as they hauled away the girls.

Eventually, it was their turn.

A man picked up Cassy. She tried to hold on to Madeline, but her hand slipped away. She screamed out for her, then she was out of the truck and out of sight of the only friend she had.

The man carried her under her arm. She tried to fight it, but the man didn't even react. She gave up. She was tired, and she was hungry, and she was thirsty — and he was much bigger than her. Any thrashing she attempted would be nothing to him.

They approached a large house. It was two floors high and quite a few windows wide, with each pane of glass too dirty to see through and surrounded by mould. Moss filled the cracks of the bricks. There were no other houses around, just fields. The man carried her up a path marked by weeds and through a splintered doorframe.

The inside of the house smelt like expired food and body odour. He took her across a corridor, up another set of steps and along another corridor. The plaster was cracked. The paint had faded. Damp covered the ceiling.

He took her into a room, empty but for a metal bed frame and a stained mattress.

He placed her on the floor. Put a chain around her ankle.

She stared at the chain, her eyes widening. She tried to pull on it, but it was attached to the bed, which was screwed into the ground.

There was no escaping.

The man stood over her. Grinned. Happy with what he'd done. Like a fisherman, marvelling at the big fish he'd just caught.

The man left, chuckling.

She was alone.

She pulled on the chain. Pulled on the bed.

She screamed, but the scream just became one of many.

Eventually, the man came back. He had what looked like a dog bowl. In it was some mashed-up food; she couldn't tell what it was. He put it in front of her. He also placed a half-empty bottle of water next to it. The liquid was murky.

She was too hungry to be fussy. She shovelled the food into her mouth with her hands. Drank down the water.

A few minutes later she was sick over the stone floor.

Despite the sunny day outside, the floor was cold. Her knees were cut, and she did not remember how that had happened.

She was still so hungry.

She wondered if Madeline was okay.

She wondered what would happen to her in this room.

She wondered if the other girls were just as scared as her.

They brought no more food to her in the following hours. Darkness came and went and, by the morning, she was painfully hungry.

She didn't sleep properly. She fell in and out of restless slumber. Never able to relax, but too tired to remain awake.

Men in some kind of military uniform occasionally walked past the open door to her room. She'd hear girls scream in adjacent rooms, then these men would leave with smiles on their faces.

Sometimes the men would stop at her door and look in, as if examining her. As if considering something. Then they would move on.

She wondered what would happen if any of those men didn't move on.

She wondered how long it would be until she found out.

And she wondered what she'd done to deserve this.

LIVERPOOL, ENGLAND

CHAPTER SIXTY-THREE

ANOTHER DREAM, ANOTHER TORMENT.

Another reason for Sullivan to hate himself.

But this time, he was not inside his body. He was standing in the corner of the room, watching himself holding the knife.

He was in his target's family home. A place of safety. A place that Sullivan had infiltrated upon instruction from government officials. He did not know who this man was or what he had done. He would never know.

It was not his job to know.

He would hope it was a bad person, but he wasn't a naïve young man at the beginning of his career anymore. He knew better. He knew it would be a bad person from the government's point of view. From someone in power.

Sullivan had learnt that the more power someone has, the less he could trust them.

Nevertheless, the target's body lay on the floor, his throat slit. As Sullivan watched the other version of himself confirm the kill, a cry drew his attention to a child, standing in the doorway, rigid through shock.

"Don't!" he begged himself. "Don't!"

He tried to restrain his doppelgänger, but he was unable to move. He could do nothing but relive the memory, watching as the Jay Sullivan of old turned to a child gripped with fear, the knife ready.

The hardest part of watching this was knowing how it would all end. He'd been there. He knew that he would murder this child.

He begged and pleaded with his former self.

How could this have been him? It was so long ago. From a time he had forgotten. When a different person filled his body. When a different mind controlled him.

The Jay Sullivan of his memory turned to the Jay Sullivan being forced to watch. Grinned. Then turned back to the child.

"Please..." Sullivan begged.

He wept.

He didn't care.

Cry, he told himself.

Go ahead.

It's fine.

He'd never allowed himself to show such weakness, but now he did.

It was too much not to.

He didn't wish that he could turn away. He wanted to, but that wasn't his wish.

No, he wished he could stop it. Make it happen another way.

The kid would not be able to faithfully recall Sullivan's appearance to the police. He was traumatised. Why didn't he just let the boy live? Even if the child gave a statement that led to a description that led back to him, people in power wouldn't allow Sullivan to be caught. He would be fine.

"You'll be okay, you don't need to do this," Sullivan urged. "He can live. You won't get caught."

But that wasn't the policy they had taught him to live by.

No witnesses. That was always the instruction.

He was a professional.

But he had never wanted to be.

He was sixteen when his dad killed his mum.

He was eighteen when a man saw an angry young orphan they could manipulate.

They taught him to fight and kill before he learnt right from wrong.

His parents had spent too much time arguing to teach him ethics. He was just doing what he was taught. He knew no different.

But that did not make him feel like he was due forgiveness. That child would never get to see what kind of adult he'd become.

Sullivan hadn't known better. They had brainwashed him. They had taught him their version of life like it was gospel, and he lived his life as an assassin because that's the life they made for him.

Could he make a different life? Could he be something else?

No. He'd tried that.

"Dad."

A voice.

Behind him.

He was able to turn around. To look at his daughter. Seventeen years old. The age she was when he last saw her, now a killer herself.

But this figment of his imagination didn't appear evil.

She smiled at him. She'd been brainwashed too. And it looked like she understood.

"Dad, you have to wake up," she said.

"What? Wake up?"

"You have to save Cassy."

"I lost her. I'm dead."

299

She smiled and shook her head warmly. "Oh, Dad. You're not dead. Just broken."

He said nothing.

Just mulled those words over and over.

You're not dead.

Just broken.

Beep.

Beep.

Beep.

The repetitive noise of a machine interrupted his unconscious.

She was right.

It was time to wake up.

ODESSA, UKRAINE

CHAPTER SIXTY-FOUR

THE MONITOR BEEPED A STEADY HEARTBEAT.

Sullivan woke up.

His chest didn't hurt. They must have given him something for it. Done something. Helped him.

But everything else hurt. Ached. His legs, his arms... his muscles felt like a burden. They had bandaged his leg where the bullet had scraped him.

Hang on...

They?

Where was he?

He sat up. He was in a hospital room. He looked around, alarmed.

He wasn't dead. How was he not dead?

He was happy to have died. He was content and ready to accept the end.

He noticed a blood transfusion leading to an artery. He must have washed up on the shore or something. Someone saved his life.

Then the real reason for his alarm gripped him — he was in a hospital.

A public hospital.

There would be records of him attending. Someone could track him. He'd gone dark, and he wanted to stay that way. He could not allow himself to stay here any longer. It was not safe. Not just from Hugo; he could be attacked by anyone seeking vengeance, or anyone from the Falcons who decided to call off their truce.

He pulled the tube from his artery. Ripped the pads off his chest.

The heart monitor sang a consistent bleep, as if indicating that the heart had stopped working. He reached over and cut the power. The last thing he needed was a bunch of doctors and nurses streaming into the room.

He swivelled and placed his feet on the floor. It was cold on the soles of his feet. He stood. His leg stung from the bullet scrape. His muscles throbbed.

He'd endured worse.

He shoved the hospital gown off, finding his clothes in a pile on a chair beside his bed. He put them on, quickly. If he was to walk through the hospital in a gown, he would look too conspicuous.

He poked his head out of the door. Looked around. A nurse walked down the corridor, so he ducked back inside, and waited for her to pass.

Once she had, he walked out of the room and into the corridor. He had a slight limp, but it would go once he was used to the pain in his leg. For now, he just had to leave.

He did not take the lift, not wanting to be trapped. He ran to the stairs and descended a floor.

The sound of conversation grew louder. A group of doctors and nurses stood outside on the stairs further below. He couldn't risk walking past them. They may recognise him, and he did not want to hurt anyone. He opened the door to the next floor. A nurse came from the corridor to his right, so he walked straight on.

A doctor approached, so he stepped into the nearest room.

A patient lay asleep.

A hooded jacket lay atop a pile of clothes. He took it, put it on, and pulled the hood up. Walked to the door, looked out.

A doctor and nurse passed.

He moved back into the room. Shut the door. Waited.

"Hey," came a voice from behind him.

He ignored it.

"Hey, how did you get here?"

Sullivan recognised that voice.

Bemused, he turned to the patient he'd thought was fast asleep in their bed.

He recognised the face.

With his mind working at half-speed, it took longer than it should have, but he knew the man in the bed.

It was Charles.

CHAPTER SIXTY-FIVE

"You," Sullivan growled.

No. Stop it. He had to refrain from being that person.

He didn't want to attack anyone. He didn't want to hurt people anymore. However much they deserved it, he needed to stay calm.

But this man lost Cassy. Without this man's interjection, without his cowardly actions, Cassy would not be gone.

Sullivan strode to the side of the bed, looking down at the man responsible for this mess.

Charles' arm and leg were in a cast. His face was bruised. He was connected to a heart monitor machine, and other various equipment.

"I should end your life right now," Sullivan stated, hoping that saying it aloud would stop his anger from following through on his threat.

"I know..." Charles answered, as if appeasing Sullivan's wrath would somehow quell it.

It didn't.

"So what happened to you?" Sullivan asked, spite dripping from his words.

"I was hit by a car."

"How lovely."

"At least, that's what they tell me."

"Well, isn't karma a bitch?"

"I really am sorry. I didn't mean to–"

"Don't. Just... don't."

Sullivan scowled down upon the wretched man's face.

He looked sorry. But sorry didn't excuse anything.

And, just as that thought settled on him, the irony became apparent.

He had wanted to apologise to Stacey. He wanted her to hear it, he wanted her to accept it. But he was being just as unforgiving as she had been.

Maybe there was no forgiveness. Maybe no one deserved it.

Maybe it was best if he just left.

Sullivan turned to go.

"Wait!"

He paused by the door. Looked back at Charles. What could he possibly have to say to him?

"I don't want to hear an apology," Sullivan said. "It does nothing. It never has. Just leave me be."

"That's not it! I mean, I am sorry, but, there's one more thing..."

Sullivan sighed. The last thing he wanted to do was hang around here, talking to this man, but a group of doctors and nurses had accumulated in the corridor. It wasn't like he could go anywhere soon.

"I don't think there's anything more we have to say to each other."

"There is, I..." Charles coughed. Wheezed. Struggled against his injuries.

Sullivan waited, watching Charles expectantly.

"The truck..." Charles attempted. "The one the girl was on..."

"Her name is Cassy."

Charles coughed again. Sullivan tried to stay patient.

"I saw the truck go," Charles said.

"That's wonderful."

"No, that's not — just listen."

"What?"

The doctors and nurses had passed. It was time to go. He opened the door.

"I saw the licence plate," Charles blurted out.

Sullivan didn't move. His head slowly turned back to Charles. Had he said what he thought he had said?

"I don't know if it'll help," Charles continued. "It was a British licence plate, and I don't know if that makes it easier, but... I memorised it."

He had memorised the licence plate.

A heavy burden fell off Sullivan, gliding off him like a waterfall.

If Charles was in fact correct, Cassy would not be lost. He could somehow track the vehicle. He could still stand a chance of saving her.

If he could find out where the brothel was that the truck had gone to...

He could go to the authorities, but they probably already knew. Hugo would have paid up in all the right places. They'd just alert Hugo that he had to evacuate the brothel before police arrived.

He would have to go himself. He would have to do it all alone, though he wasn't sure if he could. The Jay Sullivan of old would manage. He would tear that place apart.

Was he really ready to enter war again?

Stupid question.

Of course he was.

It would be bloody. It would be messy. It would be utter carnage.

He could not hold back, and he did not want to.

"What is the licence plate?" Sullivan asked.

Charles told him. Sullivan memorised it. Repeated it to himself again and again.

"Thank you," Sullivan said, and turned to go.

"What are you going to do?" Charles asked.

"Sort them out."

"You don't have to. You could just leave it. Live a happy life."

"Like you have?"

"I'm alive, aren't I? I may have made some questionable decisions, but I can live with it so long as I am alive."

This man...

Dead wife.

Sold out child to child trafficker.

Sold out Sullivan for a new life.

He'd taken every cowardly opportunity he could to live a free life, but Sullivan didn't care about a free life — not if that was the cost.

"Goodbye, Charles," he said.

He pulled the hood over his face and continued to sneak out of the hospital.

CHAPTER SIXTY-SIX

Sullivan found a payphone.

Armed with nothing but a licence plate and unbreakable determination, he dialled in the number of the one man he could rely on when it came to vehicles.

"Hello?" responded a tired voice.

"Marty, this is Sullivan," Sullivan said.

"Oh hey — *not.*"

"What?"

"Yeah, you hung up on me. Remember that, like five days ago? Possibly six, I dunno, my sleep pattern is kind of out of whack."

"Sorry about that. I need some help."

"Oh, that's how it is, huh? Ignore me for years, then ring me up, get some help, then hang up, then ring me up again and tell me–"

"Marty, please, I don't have time for this."

He looked around. The sun was setting. He thought about what Cassy might be subjected to at that very moment.

"Fine! But this is the last time, I swear. I ain't just someone you can use and–"

"If I give you a licence plate, would you still be able to track its whereabouts in Ukraine?"

"In Ukraine, huh?" Marty suddenly seemed to brighten up. "Ah, sweet, you brought me a challenge! Hit me with it."

Sullivan told him the licence plate.

"Brill. Now just uno momento..."

Sullivan tapped his foot.

"Right," Marty said, after what seemed like an age. "This truck is frequently going from Southampton to Odessa. Like, it does the same trip every few months. Normally arrives back from Ukraine within a week. It's registered to a transportation business."

"Where was the last place a traffic cam picked it up?"

"A few minutes ago, pulling into a port in Odessa."

So the truck had dropped her off already.

"Where did it go before that?"

"Hang on."

"As quick as you can, Marty."

"You're asking me to spread across borders, man, it will take a bit of doing."

The tapping of a few keys came through the phone.

"It's driven up a road called the E95. Next one is E471."

Sullivan recognised them as names of roads in Ukraine. It had been years since he'd used them, but he remembered them.

"They ended up in Lviv. It's kinda north west Ukraine, near the Poland border, near to Slovakia."

"Anything more precise than that? Anywhere particular in Lviv?"

"Yeah, it drove onto the P31. P32. P26. E40. This is a long journey, man."

"Where was the last sighting?"

"On the P40. It turned into a wooded area and disappeared."

Into a wooded area.

That was it.

"Are there any buildings in that wooded area? Big buildings, like away from any others. Looks rundown. Like you wouldn't want to live in it."

"What are you looking for?"

"The kind of building that would be a brothel full of trafficked girls, Marty."

"You getting me to do all this so you can have a good time?"

Sullivan groaned. "No, I'm tracking a girl I'm trying to help. That's why I want to be quick."

"Ah, I see, well — oh, wait. Bingo. I've found it. This has got to be it."

Sullivan smiled. The first smile he'd managed in a while.

"Tell me how to get there."

"No problem. Hey, by the way, did you ever find out any more about that Hugo Jones guy?"

As he listened to Marty and memorised the directions, he thought about his next steps.

The weapons he would need to acquire.

Grenades.

Bullet-proof vest.

A map.

And, most importantly, a thick pair of chain-cutters — capable of both breaking chains and causing damage to an opponent.

He knew where to get these things from. He'd acquired such items plenty of times all those years ago, when he needed supplies and he needed them quickly. Being abroad was not an obstacle.

Within an hour, he had what he needed.

He stole a car and followed the map.

It looked like a ten-hour journey to where he needed to go. He was confident he would cut that down by at least two hours.

He would hit them in the dead of night.

He was on his way.

He was going to war.

CHAPTER SIXTY-SEVEN

Jay Sullivan was not a man of subtlety, and for that, Hugo was grateful.

As soon as the ship had re-docked and he had walked into Odessa, he overheard the gossiping voyeurs. A man had been washed ashore covered in blood, and that people were still talking about it meant it can't have happened too long ago.

The next logical step had been the hospital.

Again, Sullivan hadn't been difficult to find. Doctors and nurses were also gossiping about a man who was washed ashore with a bullet wound. What's more, this patient had somehow disappeared.

Hugo headed in the direction of the mayhem, followed by an entourage of men with concealed guns; he wasn't taking any chances. Their instructions were shoot on sight, deal with the aftermath later.

He'd had enough. Besides, he had the money, the power, and the contacts to hush up any kind of chaos.

But, just as expected, the bed was empty.

Hugo kicked nothing. He did not swear. He'd displayed his temper enough. This time he leant against the edge of the bed.

Stretched his body. Twisted his neck. Allowed his anger to gather just beneath the surface.

His men backed away. To them, this was even worse. It was like filling a balloon with more and more air until it expands and expands and cannot take the air anymore, so it explodes with a bang.

Everyone was waiting for that bang.

Then one of his men dared to approach Hugo, just so they can say something quietly in his ear.

"Charles is here."

"What? Who's that?"

"The man who you allowed on the boat in exchange for Jay Sullivan."

"Ah, yes, I see. Why do I care?"

"Because Sullivan was seen walking out of his room."

Hugo straightened up. Now why would Sullivan want to speak to Charles?

Unless Charles was able to tell him something...

"Take me there."

Hugo followed, his men trailing behind him, until they arrived outside a room where, sure enough, Charles was in a bed, connected to machines.

"Wait outside," he told his men, and he walked in alone.

Charles' eyes were closed. His heartbeat monitor beeped a steady beep. He had all kinds of tubes connected to him, some going into his body, one leading to an oxygen mask.

Hugo pulled up a chair. Sat with his right foot on the knee of his left leg, clasped his hands together, and spoke.

"Why are you here?"

Charles' eyes opened. Widened. Turned to look at Hugo.

Hugo enjoyed the terror in Charles' eyes. He savoured the fear he was inciting. He had never grown tired of that look. How ever many times he saw it, it made him realise just how powerful he was; that just sitting there was enough to make a grown man fill with dread.

"Hugo?" he exclaimed.

"Yes. I'm worried about you, my friend. What happened?"

"I – I was hit by a car."

"Oh, I am so sorry. It pains me to see you like this. I will ensure they give you the best care possible, you have my word."

Charles seemed to relax a little. Not fully, but enough that he seemed assured Hugo didn't know he'd spoken to Jay Sullivan.

Hugo stood. Ran his fingers down the tube connected to Charles' oxygen mask.

"I wonder what this does."

"I – I think it's feeding me oxygen."

"Why is that?"

"One of my lungs is damaged. They said it was just a prec–"

Hugo squeezed it.

Charles immediately struggled to breathe, trying to take in breaths of air, but only wheezing.

Hugo released his grip.

"Ah, so that's what it does."

Charles turned his head to Hugo. There was that look of terror again.

"What did you tell Jay Sullivan?" he asked.

"Jay Sullivan? I–"

Hugo squeezed the tube. Again, Charles suffocated. The heart rate monitor beeped faster.

Hugo grinned.

A nurse outside was trying to get in. His men would ensure she had no chance.

He released the tube again.

"What did you tell Jay Sullivan?"

"Nothing, he just–"

Hugo squeezed again.

This time he held it for longer.

Long enough that Charles could really fear that Hugo would not stop.

Hugo let it go.

"What did you tell Jay Sullivan?"

"I didn't, it was just–"

Hugo went to squeeze again.

"Fine, Fine!" Charles said. "I gave him the licence plate of the truck with the girl in, but that was all, I swear, that was all. And, I mean, what can he do with a licence plate?"

Hugo dropped his head. Clenched his jaw.

"Everything," he snarled.

He squeezed the tube again.

This time, he did not release his grip.

He held onto it as Charles squirmed and thrashed. Charles entered a seizure and his heartbeat monitor sped up quicker and quicker and quicker until there was no beat at all. Just a flatline.

Hugo ripped the tube away and tore it in two, ensuring that when the doctors entered in a moment, there would be no easy fix.

He left the room. His men followed. Finally, a stream of nurses and doctors entered the room.

Security approached, but when they saw what they were facing, they backed down.

"Get me a car," he told the man next to him. "We're going to Lviv."

317

OUTSIDE OF LVIV, UKRAINE

CHAPTER SIXTY-EIGHT

Cassy was lonely, she was tired, and she was cold.

The room had stone walls and a stone floor, and it felt like a box of ice. Many spiders had made homes in the corners of the room, and most of them were now dead. The chain around her ankle was tight. The sound of dripping taunted her.

She huddled her knees to her chin and wrapped her arms around them. She shivered, and she rubbed her skin, trying to keep warm.

She had seen a lot of men walk past her room. Sometimes, they would stop and look at her, then carry on. Sometimes they would look at her for a while, as if studying her. They would look her up and down. They would often smile.

But they never came in to see her.

Yet, somehow, when she heard a distant tap of light feet, she knew they were for her.

She had no idea how she knew it.

The taps were gentle, a person with an unnaturally light step. Walking like a metronome. A little shuffle in their walk.

They paused out of sight.

She waited, dreading to see what appeared.

A man stepped into the doorway.

Thin. Gangly. Skin wrapped around his bones. A lecherous smile. Flat hair parted to the side.

A grin that made her body stiffen.

She scampered away from him. Pushing herself up against the far wall.

It didn't help. Was she thinking she could get away from him? She was fixed to the ground.

He stepped in. Slowly. Walking particularly and intentionally.

But he didn't approach her.

He just sat on the bed.

Watching.

Her body relaxed a little, but she remained tense.

Maybe this man would not hurt her.

Maybe he was here to be nice.

Maybe he would free her.

No. She was being deluded. There was no one coming to rescue her.

"Are you all right?" the man asked, his voice unusual. He had an accent. She noticed a burn mark on his neck.

She didn't answer.

"I imagine you must be quite scared," he acknowledged.

She hesitated. Nodded. He seemed friendly.

"Am I your first?"

She grew confused. Her first what?

"You are new here, aren't you?"

She paused. Nodded again.

"What is your name?"

She thought about whether to answer. Somehow, her lips opened, and her shaking voice came out.

"... Cassy."

The man gasped. "What a lovely name. Your parents must love you very much."

She looked down.

She had no parents.

She had no family left at all.

"Oh, I am so sorry," the man said. "You don't have any parents, do you?"

She shook her head.

"That is a terrible, terrible tragedy. I have no family, either. It's not nice. Is it?"

She shook her head.

"How about, for the next hour or so, I be your family? Would you like that?"

She tensed again.

Something about him seemed... off.

She didn't want him to be her family. She wanted her own family back.

Grandad.

Grandma.

She wanted to be back on the farm, making songs with her guitar and playing on her swing.

"This is a strange place, isn't it? I imagine you really miss your home."

She did not answer him.

"Would you like me to tell you how you can feel better? How you can make it all okay?"

He reached a hand out and placed it on her ankle. He rubbed his hand up and down her shin, stroking her affectionately.

She nodded.

He said he would make it all okay.

Maybe he knew how she could get home.

"The secret is to forget about it," he said.

She frowned. That wasn't what she expected him to say.

His rubbing of her leg grew more vigorous, more enthusiastic.

"You are never going home again. This is your home now. And the sooner you accept that, the sooner you can stop whining and crying. The sooner you can stop all those pathetic reactions that serve no purpose but to annoy the fuck out of everyone."

His voice was no longer kind.

It was louder. More growly. More evil.

His hand gripped her ankle. He held hard, digging his thumbs in, and she yelped with pain.

"Who are you?" she cried.

"Oh, I am ever so sorry. I didn't introduce myself, did I?"

He stood.

Took off his belt.

Slid off his shirt.

"My name," he told her, "is Phillipe."

CHAPTER SIXTY-NINE

THE HOUSE WAS JUST AS SULLIVAN EXPECTED.

Rundown. Weeds covering the path. Three bulky men standing outside the entrance.

He parked a short distance away; close enough that those three men could see his car, but far enough away that they would have to leave their post to investigate it.

At first, they just stared. Spoke among themselves, asking if anyone knew why this car might be there.

This allowed Sullivan to ready himself.

He had everything he needed. A bullet-proof vest over a loose t-shirt. Trousers that gave him the freedom to run. Trainers that supported his feet.

He took a few pills for his heart. It felt fine, but the last thing he needed was for it to play up amid battle.

The house had two floors, but it was wide. He'd have to make his way through the corridors, checking every bedroom, taking on anyone he came across.

If it was anything as he imagined, there would be security at the beginning. Maybe a kitchen. A bathroom. But they would use most rooms as bedrooms, probably with young girls chained to something. Possibly drugged so they don't react to what's done to them.

Cassy was in there, he knew it. There was no other possibility.

"Identyfikuyte sebe!" one man shouted.

They each readied their guns and approached, cautiously.

Sullivan breathed in, held, and released.

In, held, released.

In, held, released.

He had to stay calm. Stay calculated. Think things through. Rely on his immediate reactions.

This would have been nothing back in the day.

He was weaker now, but only in his mind. Only if he allowed himself to be. It was all psychological.

"Khto ty!" the man shouted.

Sullivan looked to the passenger seat beside him, at a large metal chain-cutter, that he tucked into the back of his belt. Strong enough to destroy a chain, but also big enough and heavy enough to cause damage in a fight.

He tucked the knife into his sock.

He held the grenade and watched the three men approach. He needed them to be in the right place. Far enough away from the house that the grenade would hurt none of the girls, yet far enough away from him that the grenades would not damage him or the car.

He needed that car for his getaway.

He waited.

They gained ground. They aimed their guns.

This was it. No turning back. His life for Cassy's, if that's what it took.

He opened the window.

"Here we go."

He held the grenade. Took off the pin. Threw it.

It landed by the feet of the approaching men. They saw what it was and tried to run, but it was too late.

It exploded, and pieces of them scattered among the fields and trees.

Sullivan leapt from the car.

People inside sure would have heard it. They would get ready for a fight, just as he had.

There was no need for subtlety now.

CHAPTER SEVENTY

Sullivan charged forward, sprinting across the grass and to the entrance.

The instant he arrived at the doorway, a security guard peered out. Sullivan upper cut the man with his chain-cutters, and blood splattered over the walls like a Rorschach test.

He brought the chain-cutters down into the man's neck hard enough to crush his oesophagus.

The corridor took him to the right. He heard heavy metal music pounding out of a room. Loud enough to disguise his grand entrance, it would seem.

In this room were another two men — one with a skinhead, one with a mohawk.

Huh. Didn't know those were still in fashion.

They rushed out as soon as they saw Sullivan. He ran toward them until they were in close proximity and stayed there, ensuring he was too close for them to aim their machine guns at him. So long as he stayed in their personal space, they could not get a good shot. They could try to shoot at an angle, but the fireback of their weapons would destroy their aim and send them off balance, possibly even breaking their wrist.

Skinhead tried to hit Sullivan with the base of his gun. Sullivan ducked it, kicked out Mohawk's leg and sent Skinhead to the floor with a strike on his kneecap. He pounded Skinhead's skull with the chain-cutters twice; this was all he managed before he saw Mohawk getting to his feet again.

Sullivan slid to his knees and landed the chain-cutters on the knuckles of Mohawk's gun hand, forcing Mohawk to drop it.

Sullivan kicked the gun away.

He put his arms around Mohawk's waist in a rugby tackle and charged him back into his office; though office was a loose term. There was a cracked desk, a few exposed nails, and a dirty kettle.

The kettle clicked to indicate it had finished boiling.

Perfect timing, thought Sullivan. He held Mohawk down, grabbed the kettle, and poured the hot water over his target's face.

Mohawk screamed and grabbed at his skin as Skinhead stumbled to his knees. Sullivan lifted his arm back and struck his chain-cutters once again at Skinhead's skull, knocking him to the floor. Sullivan turned the desk upside down, landing it on the already crushed section of Skinhead's skull, and Skinhead twitched a few times, then ceased moving.

Mohawk tried to regather himself, but struggled to see. Sullivan took Mohawk's head and drove his right eye into an exposed nail poking from the wall.

He carried on through the corridor.

To his right, a toilet flushed behind a door. He waited against the wall.

The door opened. A man walked out. Big, tattooed knuckles, gun over his back. Sullivan wasted no time. He swiftly turned and forced the man backwards, taking out his legs and dropping him to the toilet.

He grabbed a clump of the man's hair, lifted the man's head

as far back as it would go, and struck it hard enough against the rim of the toilet to knock him out. He forced the man's head deep into the toilet bowl, flushed it and held him there, waiting for him to drown.

He continued past a few doors, all of them open. Some of them contained a bed and nothing else, but it wasn't long until he came to the first occupied room. A girl was attached to the bed by a chain. Dry Mascara sticking to her cheeks, a dog bowl beside her knees, and bruises on her body.

It was sickening.

It enraged Sullivan, but he had to contain it. He had to stay calm. Had to control his emotions.

He could allow nothing to void the clarity of a clear mind.

He cut her chains, then moved past another empty room to his left. To his right was a closed door. He opened it. Shelves of supplies surrounded a young guy sorting through boxes of cheap bathroom supplies. His gun rested on the floor.

The guy looked to the gun. To Sullivan. To the gun.

The guy made his move, but Sullivan got there first, kicking the gun out of reach. He knocked a box of supplies to the floor, spilling its contents. He briefly examined them and found a razor, using it to slice the man's throat.

He shut the door as he left.

A few more steps and he heard grunting. Repetitive grunting, but he couldn't tell where from.

Another empty bedroom to his right.

One to his left, with a girl on her own.

He reached the next bedroom and the source of the grunting became clear.

A girl lay on the bed, her arms splayed out and her eyelids wavering between open and closed. A man was on top of her, thrusting into a child who was too drugged up to even know, his clothes discarded by the front door.

His grunting grew louder. His thrusts became harder. His aggression became infectious.

The jacket left discarded on the floor was that of a soldier's uniform.

Any attempt to contain anger left Sullivan, and his rage intensified.

"Odpieprz sie!" the man shouted as he turned toward Sullivan.

Sullivan knew other languages well enough to know when a man was telling him to fuck off.

Sullivan didn't leave, and the man looked to the gun he had left hung over the end of the bed as a warning.

Sullivan charged forward, past the man's discarded trousers, sliding the belt from the trousers' waist. The man shouted and tried to confront Sullivan, but Sullivan had tied the belt around his neck before he could object. He pulled the man from the girl and held him against the floor with a knee in his back, pulling the belt harder and harder.

The naked bastard choked to death quicker than Sullivan had expected.

Sullivan stood, knowing his wrath was no longer contained.

He looked to the girl. She groaned and moved her head to the side, not at all aware of what had just happened. Too intoxicated to know.

He use the chain cutters to free her ankle and helped her to her feet. She stumbled, and used Sullivan balance herself.

"Get out," he told her. "Run."

She looked at him hazily, but seemed to understand well enough. She used the wall to steady herself as she stumbled forward, slowly making her way through the corridor.

Sullivan watched her go. He had tried to stay calm, but he didn't want to anymore. Every abusive bastard in this building would die, and every one of them was going to deserve it.

CHAPTER SEVENTY-ONE

THE MAN WHO CALLED HIMSELF PHILLIPE STOOD BEFORE Cassy, as naked as the day he was born. His body was bony and infantile. His dick was small. His chest was hairless.

Cassy backed up.

"You should thank me," said Phillipe. "They gave drugs to the other girls, but I told them not to drug your food. Do you know why?"

Phillipe approached her. Crouched. She pushed herself up against the wall.

"Because I want you to be aware of *everything*."

She screamed.

She'd screamed before, but not like this.

This man was not friendly like he'd initially seemed. He was scary. It was as if the more friendly he became, the scarier he was.

"How old are you, Cassy?"

She stared at him and persisted in screaming

"It's no good," Phillipe said, shaking his head, so patronising, so vindictive. "There's no one coming to help you. It's just us."

He ran his hand down her cheek. His hand was cold and coarse.

She stopped screaming, knowing he was right. She looked around the room, frantically, not sure what she was searching for, but knowing something bad was about to happen and wanting a way to stop whatever he was about to do.

"Now answer my question. How old are you, Cassy?"

"E – eleven," she stuttered.

He gasped.

"Eleven! Oh, my. What a lovely age."

He kept running his hand down her cheek. It was as if he was being affectionate — but he wasn't. He was rubbing hard, sometimes with the back of his hand, covering her whole face.

"Do you know what a virgin is, Cassy?"

She stared. Nodded, vaguely.

"Good girl. Really good girl. A tribute to your parents, honestly, it is wonderful to be in your company."

He moved his head closer, so he was inches from her. She smelt the garlic on his breath. She saw the acne scars on his skin.

"Are you a virgin, Cassy?"

She stared. Nodded.

He grinned.

"How sweet."

"Please, don't hurt me."

"Hurt you?"

"Don't touch me."

He stopped rubbing her cheek and grabbed her chin.

"Get off me," she demanded.

"Now, now, there's no need to be rude."

"Madeline! Madeline!" she cried out.

"Who the fuck is Madeline? If it's one of the other girls, I assure you she will be rather busy by now."

"Help! Please help!"

"Again, who are you calling out to help you?"

She screamed.

He laughed.

"I assure you, Cassy – there is absolutely no one in this building who has any intention of helping you."

CHAPTER SEVENTY-TWO

THAT SCREAM.

It was her.

It was Cassy; he knew it.

It came from upstairs.

He ran to the stairs and took them two at a time.

A man appeared at the top of the steps and aimed his gun. He fired downwards, and Sullivan had to back up and around the wall.

The man continued downward, and Sullivan returned to the ground floor corridor, closing the door.

He listened. Waited for footsteps.

As soon as they were close, he kicked open the door. He heard the man stumble over and reached him before he raised his gun. Sullivan's heel broke the guy's nose. His falling knee winded him.

He moved the man's head into the space between the door and the doorframe, and slammed the door hard against his cranium once, twice, then three times, just to make sure.

He made his way back up the stairs and entered the corridor. Another long, twisted route lay out in front of him, with screams of girls and moans of men creating a symphony of despair.

"Cassy!" he cried out.

Waited. Nothing.

"Cassy, where are you?"

He moved through the corridor.

Empty room to his left. Toilet to his right. A girl he didn't know in the next room to his left, bent over the bed and a man behind her with his back to Sullivan.

Sullivan pounded his chain-cutters against the man's head until the pervert was nothing but a bloody corpse.

Next was another bedroom, then another empty room, then another room with a girl who wasn't Cassy.

"Cassy, where are you?"

Nothing tangible responded. Just more screams.

Cassy's screams.

He could be mistaken, but he wasn't. He knew it was her.

He knew it.

"Cassy, talk to me, where are you?"

He kept going through the corridor.

Empty bedroom.

Girl alone.

Empty bedroom.

Empty bedroom.

Girl crying.

Girl alone.

Girl being fucked.

Kill the man, move on.

Until he came to the final room.

The room where the screams grew deafening.

He placed the chain-cutters on his belt, tucked his knife by his side, slowed down, and approached.

He saw her. Backed up against the wall. The dainty arse of a nude, scrawny bloke standing in front of her.

Cassy saw him and they locked eyes. The man, realising they were no longer alone, looked over his shoulder.

Sullivan froze.

No. It couldn't be.

Him?

Phillipe opened his arms as if about to embrace an old friend, his poorly endowed cock dangling off his tightly wrapped skin.

"Jay Sullivan," he acknowledged. "This is a delightful surprise. Please, do join us."

CHAPTER SEVENTY-THREE

WAS THIS REAL?

Was Cassy imagining it?

The creepy man who called himself Phillipe turned away from her. Looked at him too. Spoke to him.

"Jay Sullivan. This is a delightful surprise. Please, do join us."

Before she could understand what had happened, Sullivan had run in, grabbed Phillipe by the throat, and pushed him up against the wall.

Phillipe did not stop smiling. Even when Sullivan stuck a knife in his gut, he smiled.

"This time," Sullivan growled, "you will not survive."

Sullivan stuck the knife in again.

He had a look on his face Cassy had never seen. Fear quickly replaced her relief, and she could do nothing but stare at Sullivan sticking his knife into Phillipe's abdomen again, and again, and again, then putting his knife to Phillipe's throat and dragging it across like he was sawing through wood. Blood splattered over Sullivan's face, but he barely blinked. He slit the throat again, and again, as if he was really, really making sure, his expression not changing at all from this strange, contorted mess of anger and wrath.

Finally, he stopped, and pulled the body out of the room so Cassy didn't have to stare at it. He took a moment before reappearing in the doorway, his skin and his shirt bloodier than it was bare.

She was so scared. This was Sullivan, but he'd just killed this man... would he hurt her?

He blinked. Wiped the blood off his face and stared at her.

"Are you okay?" he asked. His voice changed. His face was nice again, like she remembered it. Covered in other men's death, but still friendly, like he was at the farm.

She cried.

Sullivan rushed forward and fell to his knees.

"Oh, God, I'm so sorry," he told her. "I'm so, so sorry."

He hugged her. She cried, and he held her, just as he had done in the car park of the pub. He held her and let her feel all those emotions she didn't understand; held her and assured her it was okay now. He was back. He had her. She was saved.

And she believed it.

He put his knife in his sock and took some big metal contraption from his belt. He placed it on the chains attached her ankle and he pressed down with all his might.

The chain broke. Although it was still around her ankle, the chain link was broken, and she was free. She was no longer attached to the bed.

"Did he do anything to you?" Sullivan asked. "Did he... hurt you?"

She shook her head.

"He said he was going to, but then... you came."

Sullivan's face, welled up with emotion, looked so relieved.

"Come on, we have to go," he told her.

"But – but what about Madeline?"

"What?"

"She's my friend."

"Forget it, we need to leave before anyone else turns up."

"But the other girls, they... They are stuck here too..."

Sullivan looked into her eyes. She could tell he was eager to leave; so was she. But he was here. She was safe.

"Fine," he said, and they ran to the next room, and he cut their chains too. And the next, and the next, freeing every girl.

Cassy looked at every face she came across, but she couldn't find the one she was searching for anywhere. Madeline was not there.

She hoped this was because she had already been freed. That she had already escaped.

She dreaded to think what else may have happened to her.

Sullivan handed the chain-cutters to Cassy to free the last few girls while he did a final check.

"Free the rest. I'll check it's safe."

Sullivan knew it was safe. He'd killed everyone. He just didn't want to take any risks.

Must be thorough. Must be sure.

Cassy ran went to the final few rooms. Cutting the chains was hard and her muscles were tired, but she pushed as hard as she could and manage to free them. The girls fled from the house, with the stronger girls helping the girls who were too drugged to understand.

Sullivan looked around, checking there was no one left that could hurt these girls. There wasn't.

He breathed a sigh of relief, unaware that Hugo Jones' car was pulling up outside the house.

CHAPTER SEVENTY-FOUR

THE DRIVER BROUGHT THE CAR TO A STOP. HE, AND THE
other two men in the car with Hugo, said nothing. They didn't
look at him. None of them dared.

No one wanted to be the first to break the silence.

The remnants of an explosion marked the ground. Bodies
piled outside the door. The inside of the corridor, as far as
Hugo could see it, was marked with blood.

And, most infuriating of all, girls fled from the house.
There'd be a moment, then another would run out. Then
another. Then another. As if they were being freed in some
kind of rhythm.

Hugo was beyond furious. He tried deep breathing. Tried
clasping his fingers. Tried biting his lip.

"Kill him," he said.

The others finally looked at Hugo.

"Go in there and bring me out his body."

His men looked to each other and, without another word,
nodded. They walked out of the car, arming themselves with
shotguns and pistols.

They moved to the door. Paused. Glanced at each other. Entered.

Hugo stepped out of the car. Removed his suit jacket. Moved forward slowly, inspecting the devastation.

Next to the marked explosion was an unrecognisable limb.

"Oh, for pity's sake."

He heard gunshots from inside the house.

They'd found him.

Hugo stood back, watching the door. Waiting. Anticipating Sullivan's body to be dragged out at any moment.

The gunshots stopped.

He waited, listening intently to the silence. What was taking them so long? Surely it didn't take three men that long to carry a body down?

But none of his men appeared.

Then another girl ran out. And another.

He grabbed one girl by the throat. Squeezed. Looked into her pale, bruised face, curling his lips over his teeth, lowering his eyes into hers.

Who the hell did she think she was?

No one left without his say so.

No one.

But a shadow distracted him. He loosened his grip, and the girl ran off.

The shadow came from inside the corridor, growing smaller against the wall, and Hugo saw the body of Jay Sullivan.

Unfortunately, Sullivan was not dead, and Hugo's men were not there.

He tutted. How agitating. His men were bloody useless.

Sullivan walked out of the house, stepping over the corpses, and stood, watching Hugo. Hands in his pocket, a smug-as-shit look on his face.

"It's done," he said. "It's over. Give it up."

This only made Hugo more determined. More angry. More ruthless.

He pulled his sleeves up. Undoing his left cuff, rolling it up, then undoing his right and rolling that up just the same.

"Not quite," he said.

Sullivan sighed.

"Enough," Sullivan insisted. "Enough of this. I'm tired. You've lost."

Hugo shook his head. "I don't think you quite realise who you're messing with."

"I don't think you quite realise what I've done!" Sullivan said, raising his voice.

How dare anyone ever raise their voice to Hugo.

"It's over!" Sullivan repeated. "There's no one left. Your men are dead. The girls are free. It's just you. Let it go. You have lost."

Hugo shook his head. Stepped forward.

"I don't lose."

CHAPTER SEVENTY-FIVE

THE FINAL GIRL RAN FROM THE HOUSE, AND CASSY WAS THE only one left. She was happy Sullivan was here, she was pleased the girls had escaped, but a feeling of sickness still remained — where was Madeline?

Madeline might have family who were waiting for her, worried sick by her absence. Her parents could probably be phoning the police every day, maybe even appearing on the news, beseeching her captor. But the house was empty, and Cassy could not stay there any longer. It was so full of death. She ran, ignoring all the remnants she stepped over, trying not to cry as she did.

She arrived at the door to find it blocked by Sullivan, who stood still, filling the door frame.

"Jay?" she asked.

Sullivan stepped forward. He hadn't noticed her.

"Let it go," he said to someone outside the house. "You've lost."

Cassy stepped out from behind him and felt dread clutch her chest once more. It was the man who'd taken her from Charles's apartment.

"I don't lose," said the man.

She stayed behind Sullivan, putting her hands on his leg. She tugged on his shirt to get his attention.

"Please, can we go?" she asked.

Sullivan looked down at her.

To the bad man.

To Cassy.

Then back to the bad man.

"I'm taking this girl home," he said. "It's over."

He took hold of Cassy's hand and walked toward a car, ignoring the bad man.

"You think that's how it is?" the bad man ranted, his face red and full of rage. "You think I'll just let you walk away?

They ignored him. Once they reached the car, Sullivan opened the passenger door and helped her in.

"You think I won't come after her?"

This seemed to do something to Sullivan. She waited for him to sit in the driver's seat, but he didn't. He just stood there, looking down at her.

"You think I won't find her the minute you have your back turned? You think I won't put her through this again, maybe something worse?"

"Please, Jay," Cassy begged. "Please, can we just go? I don't want to be here anymore. This is a bad, bad place."

"I have plenty of places like this. And next time you won't find her. Hundreds of men just passing through will fuck and destroy her. Soldiers. Politicians. Scum of the Earth. All of them will have a go."

"Jay, please."

He still didn't move.

Why wasn't he moving? Why wasn't he getting in the car and driving her away?

"I want to go," she insisted.

He seemed to give in. Seemed to accept Cassy's pleas and gave in to her attempts.

That was until the bad man spoke just that one last time.

"I have plenty of Phillipes, Sullivan. Plenty of them, waiting for a girl like this."

Sullivan's face changed. Like it did when he came in to save her. Turning red like it did when he hurt that man.

"Stay here," Sullivan told her.

"No, please, come back!" Cassy cried, but it was no good.

He shut the door.

Turned his back on the car, and on her.

"No!" she shouted.

He stepped toward the bad man.

She battered against the window, pounding it with all her fading might. She just wanted to go. She didn't want to stay here any longer.

Sullivan looked back at her. Held her gaze. Smiled.

This seemed to comfort her, somehow.

She sat back down.

Sullivan covered his eyes for a moment, then pointed at Cassy.

She understood what this meant.

Sullivan was indicating that she must cover her eyes and not uncover them until Sullivan told her to, no matter what she heard.

So this was what she did.

CHAPTER SEVENTY-SIX

IT WAS JUST THE WAY IT SEEMED TO GO.

Once again, Sullivan would walk away with blood on his hands.

He didn't want to be a killer, but it was like telling an expert pianist that they should never play the piano.

It was what he did best. It was the only way he could ever solve a situation.

Funny, really. He'd spent so long trying not to be a killer, being plagued by nightmares of those he'd hurt, feeling the guilt of what he'd done and bemoaning the conditioning that led to him, as a young man, believing he was doing the right thing. Yet, here he was, another load of corpses piling on his conscience.

And all he still offered to the world was more death.

The building beside him was evidence of that.

Then again, what was he supposed to do? Ask them politely to let the girls go? Compromise? Contact officials who were buying expensive second homes based on the hush money Hugo had provided?

It was all he could give.

Yet, the one piece of respite, the one thing he had held onto — was that Connor, Elsie and Cassy didn't see him that way. They did not know who he was, what he'd done, or what he was capable of. They'd accepted him without judgement or question. They hadn't needed to know anything.

Connor and Elsie were gone now. Cassy was left. And she didn't need to know, and that was why he told her to cover her eyes.

He could justify Phillipe's death. Without Phillipe's demise, Cassy's childhood would have truly been ruined beyond repair. Now Phillipe was gone and there was still a childhood Cassy could salvage.

He could even justify all the deaths of those who stood in his way of rescuing Cassy and those girls.

But Hugo...

Hugo wasn't visibly hurting anyone in front of him. He wasn't an imminent threat. There was no immediate reason to take him out. Sullivan could walk away now, without killing Hugo, convinced that he had only killed those he'd had to kill.

Except, he couldn't walk away, could he?

Because Hugo was relentless. Powerful. He needed to be stopped.

And, as ever, death was what Sullivan offered the world.

But this was the bad guy, right?

But weren't they all?

Wasn't that what they'd told him when he was recruited at eighteen? That he would kill the bad guys so the good guys could be saved?

How was this any different?

"I don't want to do this," Sullivan stated.

"You just killed more of my men than I can count," Hugo retorted. "What, because the girl's watching, that's making you weak?"

He looked back at Cassy.

She kept her eyes closed, just as he'd told her. Good girl.

He took out his knife. Held it loosely in his hand, feeling its weight. His hand was so used to its handle that he could easily have been holding a spoon, or a ladle, or a child's hand.

He pleaded with himself not to use it.

He didn't listen.

"You are murder, Jay Sullivan," insisted Hugo, pacing toward him.

"No," Sullivan defied. "I don't have to be a murderer."

"Nuh-uh, listen to my words. I did not say you are a murderer. I said you are *murder*."

Sullivan gripped the knife but kept it by his side. He would only raise it if he had to.

If he *had* to.

But Hugo kept walking toward him, revealing a gun by his waist.

"It is all you are. Your personality consists of one thing."

"I'm not *murder*."

"What, you think you're also love? Compassion? Decency? Come off it! You are an assassin. It's how you were trained. And what, now you decide to spend your time fighting it?"

Hugo kept moving forward, placing his hand on his gun.

"Please don't take the gun out," Sullivan said.

"What's one more death to add?"

"I only kill the ones who attacked me or attacked the girls. If you don't attack me, I need not kill you."

"Is that what you tell yourself? Is that what will stop the nightmares?"

Sullivan exhaled a long, desperate exhale. Looked to the sky. Considered saying a prayer, but he knew no one was listening.

Hugo was around six or seven steps away now. Hugo knew Sullivan didn't have a gun — everyone knew that he detested guns.

One quick shot and Hugo would have Sullivan on the floor, and Cassy would return to Hugo's possession.

Sullivan had to kill Hugo for her.

But if he did... would that mean Hugo was right?

Was he *murder*?

"I can see it, the fight in your mind. Trying to give yourself permission. You can do nothing but listen to my taunts. Am I inside your head, Sullivan? Am I?"

He looked back at Cassy.

She had her eyes covered, but she heard everything.

What would she think of him now?

"I imagine that inside your head is not a pleasant place to be. But I'm in there, kicking shit around, fucking up all the thoughts you ignore."

The gun was out from beside Hugo's waist.

In his hand.

By his side.

Sullivan watched the gun, hoping that it would stay there, ready for the moment it didn't.

Ready to pounce.

Ready to show Hugo that he was correct.

Hugo stepped forward.

Sullivan stayed still.

"You are *murder*. You were murder when you were a teenager, you were murder when you were an adult. Tell me, what happened to your wife? Was that murder?"

"Enough!"

"All you are is a master of death."

Hugo's raised his gun arm, and Sullivan didn't waste a moment. He threw his arm up, released the knife, and watched it land in Hugo's chest.

Sullivan sprinted forward, withdrew the knife and sunk it into Hugo's stomach.

Hugo's eyes widened.

The attempt to get inside of his head, to delay his reaction long enough for Hugo to lift his gun...

It hadn't worked.

Sullivan hadn't wanted Hugo to be right.

But, as he thrusted the knife into Hugo's throat, he knew he'd had no choice.

He lay Hugo down.

Hugo's body flopped. His head turned. Looked to Sullivan.

Sullivan took the knife from Hugo's neck, and waited until he could confirm the death.

That was what an assassin did.

A master of death.

But an assassin would also flee the scene quickly.

Sullivan did not.

He stayed there a moment longer. Listening to the silence in the building behind him.

He had to go. Leave the country quickly. Someone would find the wreckage soon.

He returned to the car.

He didn't tell Cassy to take her hands away from her eyes until they were on the road, and out of sight of the house.

LOIRE VALLEY, FRANCE

CHAPTER SEVENTY-SEVEN

SULLIVAN HAD NEVER WANTED TO PUT A CHILD INTO THE system. Especially a child already so old. But he had no choice.

As much as she begged and pleaded, Cassy could not stay with Sullivan.

He had forced such a life upon Talia and look what happened. If he'd placed her somewhere where she could grow up properly, Talia may never have been taken as she had. But he still remained involved in Cassy's care as long as he needed to be, returning every day to make sure Cassy was okay at the children's home. To make sure everything was being done to provide her with a family.

Then Sullivan had decided it was taking too long, and he'd to find a family for her himself. He recalled the name of a girl Cassy had mentioned in the days following her rescue; a girl who had been a friend when she'd most needed one. He tracked this girl to the French countryside and did every check he could to find out who her family was, even risking contact with acquaintances he had distanced himself from long ago.

Madeline's family could not have been more perfect.

The mother was a counsellor who helped victims of trauma.

Considering the flashbacks and anxiety problems Cassy had been experiencing, she would need someone who understood. She was already receiving help through the best mental health services, paid for by Sullivan, but this meant the support would also be there at home.

The father was a teacher. He taught Geography and History. Two regular subjects. Nothing special. Just like she needed.

As well as Madeline, she would have a younger brother and an older sister. The older sister was already at university, studying for a law degree. The younger brother was feisty, but Cassy needed that. Someone to take care of. He knew she would be at home there.

After she had settled in, he came to visit her, asking to speak to her. The family would not let her go anywhere with him, which made him happy. They were wary, and that was good. After a bit of persuading, they let him speak to her in their garden, where they could keep watch.

Cassy was excited to see him. So excited she could barely contain herself. They sat on her new swing set as she told him everything about her new home.

"And my little brother, he has a hamster, and he let me play with it, and it bit my hand and so I called it Bitey and he said it was a good name. They got me a guitar. And they got this swing set for me, because I said I missed my old one. Do you think they'll ever let me back to the farm, Sullivan? Just to see it again."

Sullivan shook his head.

"I don't think that would be a good idea."

"What about you?" she carried on, just as enthusiastically. "Can you stay for tea? I know they'd let you. I have to take my medication first, but that's okay, the pills are to help me. Maybe we could make you visiting a regular thing, like every week. Or every month, I know you're busy. What do you think?"

Sullivan hesitated.

What an incredible girl.

She had been through a literal hell, and he could see her suffering beneath the surface — but here she was, eager to start her new life. Never to forget her old one, but ready to embrace the new.

She was stronger than he was.

Yet he still hated what he was about to say.

"I don't think I can do that. I'm sorry."

Her whole body seemed to drop.

"Oh. Why not? We don't have to have you round for tea if you don't want, we could do other things."

"No, Cassy. I'm afraid I won't be visiting at all."

"What?"

"This will be the last time you see me, I'm afraid."

"Why? No, that's not fair! You can't say that!"

Her protest came with such vehemence. Everything in her body was beseeching him not to go. She was adamant. She truly believed she could stop him from leaving.

He hated that.

"I'm a part of your old life," he said. "Not a part of your new one."

"Then I don't want my new one."

"It doesn't work like that."

"I don't want you to go, Jay, I don't want you to!"

"All I am is a reminder. Something that prompts memories of what happened. You don't need me."

"I do, I do need you! You're not a reminder, really, you're not!"

He looked to her adoptive mother in the window, looking concerned. His time with Cassy was drawing to a close, and he felt he was outstaying his welcome.

"Listen to me," he said. "I made sure you have a family that loves you. And you do. That's all I can offer, I'm afraid. I'm not a constant in your life. All I bring with me is bad news."

"I – I don't understand."

"Someday you will."

He stood up. Smiled a solemn smile. Ruffled her hair and walked toward the garden door.

He wouldn't go back through the house. He didn't want to taint it.

"Jay," she called out, just before he left.

He paused. Looked back at her.

"Don't, Cassy. I have to go."

"I know, it's just..."

She seemed to struggle over a few thoughts, attempt a few words, and then she said it.

"The bad man was wrong."

"What?"

"What he was saying. He was wrong."

"About what?"

She struggled again, then just seemed to come out and say it.

"You are not murder. You are a hero."

He smiled. Oh, how little she knew.

"Thanks," he told her.

He left. Closed the gate and moved on.

He had one more place to visit.

SWINDON, ENGLAND

CHAPTER SEVENTY-EIGHT

IT WAS JUST AS SULLIVAN HAD REMEMBERED IT. IT HAD EASILY been fifteen, twenty years, and it still looked just the same.

A perfect family home. Suburban setting. A community where everyone knew each other. A street where the kids could ride their bikes. A driveway where Sullivan and his wife would park when they visited.

You'd never have known it was the site of Grant's death.

He crossed the white picket fence and walked up the path, past the lawn, a field of daisies, a ball and a child size goal.

He paused by the door and hesitated.

Deciding to do it before he convinced himself not to, he knocked on the door.

When it opened, a bemused face looked back at him. It took Stacey a little while to recognise him. He had evidently aged a bit since last time.

Once she realised who it was, she went to close the door. Sullivan put a hand out to stop it closing.

"Go away," she demanded.

"Please, just give me two minutes."

"I will call the police."

"Go ahead. It will take the police two minutes to get here, and, like I said, that is all I need."

She opened the door slightly. Scowled at him.

"The last thing I need is some murderer harassing me. I have children here. Is there something wrong with you?"

"Yes. The same thing that was wrong with Grant. And I want to explain it to you."

"You *killed* people for a living. What is there to explain?"

"It was wrong of us to do that, but it wasn't quite that simple."

"We're not talking about forgetting to pick up milk, Jay. We are talking about cold-blooded murder."

"Please, let me explain. Then, at least you'll have a better understanding of your husband, whether or not you agree with that understanding."

This seemed to appease her. Seemed to persuade her slightly. She did not open the door any further, but she didn't shut it either.

"I'm willing to explain, if you're willing to listen."

"Make it quick."

And so he began.

He told her a story of a man.

A man who was forced into a job he didn't understand when he was young enough to be coerced.

A man who was taught to murder as if it was for the greater good and was given no option but to believe that.

A man who, at the end of his life, realised what was so very wrong about all that he had been taught.

When the man's actions caught up with him, it was too much. He had wanted none of it. But it was what they had taught him. It was all he knew.

They made him to believe that killing was not only natural, but that it was right.

That every target deserved their fate.

Murder is a big thing to pardon, and it should never be excused — but it was the people who made him think it was the right thing to do that require punishing.

All this man had ever wanted was forgiveness, as undeserving as he was.

He wanted the one he loved to understand that it did not change the man she knew.

He was made into a killer — but that had only worked because, beneath that, he had always been a fragile, damaged boy.

He told her a story of a someone who, once he realised it was wrong, the trauma was too much.

He told her about someone who couldn't cope

He told her of a person who could not look himself in the mirror.

Sullivan told her this in detail that no one else could manage, and in detail no one else could provide.

To him, it was a very familiar story.

THE BARS THAT HOLD ME IS OUT NOW

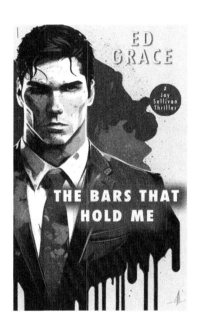

WOULD YOU LIKE A FREE BOOK?

Join Ed Grace's mailing list and get FREE and EXCLUSIVE novella that tells the story of how Jay Sullivan was recruited to be an assassin...

Join at www.edgraceauthor.com/sign-up

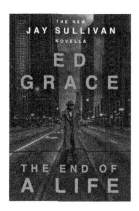

ED
GRACE

A
Jay
Sullivan
Thriller

KILL THEM
QUICKLY

ED GRACE

A
Jay
Sullivan
Thriller

A DEADLY
WEAPON

TARGET ACQUIRED

A Jay Sullivan Thriller

Printed in Great Britain
by Amazon

37113795R00219